PRAIRIE SCHOONER BOOK PRIZE IN FICTION
Editor: Hilda Raz

UNIVERSITY OF NEBRASKA PRESS | LINCOLN AND LONDON

Call Me Ahab

A SHORT STORY COLLECTION | ANNE FINGER

Manufactured in the
United States of America

Library of Congress
Cataloging-in-Publication Data
Finger, Anne.
Call me Ahab:
a short story collection /
Anne Finger.
  p. cm.
— (Prairie Schooner
book prize in fiction)
ISBN 978-0-8032-2533-6
(pbk. : alk. paper)
1. People with disabilities
—Fiction. 2. Disabilities
—Fiction. I. Title.
PS3556.I4677C36 2009
813'.54—dc22
2009004673
Set in Adobe Garamond by Bob Reitz.
Designed by R. W. Boeche.

To my mother, Mary Elizabeth Finger

Contents

Acknowledgments

This collection of short fiction could not have been written without the support and encouragement of many people. Gene Chelberg, Ben Collins, Karen Donovan, Barbara Faye Waxman Fiduccia, Mary Elizabeth Finger, Max Finger, Kenny Fries, Christopher Leland, Victoria Ann Lewis, Simi Linton, Deborah Najor, Stephen Pelton, Kevin Rashid, Nat Sobel, Brian Thorstenson, and Cecilia Woloch gave valuable feedback on these stories—and, more important, were wonderful friends. Many other friends just as dear to me (too many to list here) sustained me in countless ways through the writing of this book: thanks to all of you.

I've been fortunate to live at a time when ideas about disability are undergoing a radical change, a transformation that is reflected in these stories. I owe an enormous debt to many disability studies scholars. In particular I want to mention—although this list is by no means exhaustive—Lennard Davis, Jim Ferris, Lakshmi Fjord, Rosemarie Garland-Thompson, Carol Gill, David Hevey, Georgina Kleege, Petra Kupers,

Stephen Kuusisto, Robert McRuer, David Mitchell and Sharon Snyder, Sue Schweik, Tom Shakespeare, Alice Sheppard, and Tobin Siebers.

I'm grateful to Hilda Raz for selecting this volume as the winner of the Prairie Schooner Book Prize and appreciative of the fine editing and warmth of everyone at University of Nebraska Press.

Ismail Kadare's *Albanian Spring* introduced me to the figure of the blind marksman. Although my approach is very different from his, I drew on factual material in Leslie Fiedler's *Freaks: Myths and Images of the Secret Self* in writing "The Artist and the Dwarf." Charlotte Brontë's *Shirley* and D. F. E. Sykes and G. H. Walker's *Ben O'Bills: The Luddite* provided crucial background material for "Our Ned," as did Kirkpatrick Sale's *Rebels against the Future*. The final story in this collection, "Moby Dick, or, the Leg," not surprisingly, draws heavily on and appropriates passages from Herman Melville's great novel.

I am also deeply grateful for residencies at Hedgebrook, Yaddo, Djerassi, and Centrum, which gave me time free from distraction to work on many of these stories. Invaluable support was also provided by the Josephine Nevins Keal Fellowship, which granted me a semester's leave from teaching in the English department at Wayne State University; and by a summer faculty research fellowship and a grant from the Diversity Project, both from Wayne State University.

My mother, Mary Elizabeth Finger, taught me from childhood that the worlds of serious literature and everyday life could permeate one another by quoting Shakespeare, T. S. Eliot, Chaucer, and Ezra Pound as she carried on with the work of raising five children. Before I started kindergarten I knew that April was "the cruelest month," that one could rally oneself to scrub the toilet by declaring, "Once more into the breach, dear friends, once more . . . ," and that sometimes the evening spread itself out "against the sky like a patient etherized upon a table." I hope the love and playfulness she showed me is evident in these pages.

Thanks to the original publishers of these stories: "Goliath" originally appeared in *Southern Review* (Winter 2004); "Gloucester" in *Southern Review* (Spring 1999); "Comrade Luxemburg and Comrade Gramsci Pass Each Other at a Congress of the Second International on the 10th of March, 1912" (under a slightly different title) in *Ploughshares* (Spring 1996); "Vincent" in *Third Coast* (Spring 1995); "Helen and Frida" in *Kenyon Review* (Summer 1994); and "The Artist and the Dwarf" in *Southern Review* (Fall 1993).

Helen and Frida

I'm lying on the couch downstairs in the TV room in the house where I grew up, a farmhouse with sloping floors in upstate New York. I'm nine years old. I've had surgery, and I'm home, my leg in a plaster cast. Everyone else is off at work or school. My mother re-covered this couch by hemming a piece of fabric that she bought from a bin at the Woolworth's in Utica ("Bargains! Bargains! Bargains! Remnants Priced as Marked") and laying it over the torn upholstery. Autumn leaves—carrot, jaundice, brick—drift sluggishly across a liver-brown background. I'm watching the *Million Dollar Movie* on our black-and-white television: today it's *Singin' in the Rain*. These movies always make me think of the world that my mother lived in before I was born, a world where women wore hats and gloves and had cinched-waist suits with padded shoulders as if they were in the army. My mother told me that in *The Little Colonel* Shirley Temple had pointed her finger and said, "As red as those roses over

there," and then the roses had turned red and everything in
the movie was in color after that. I thought that was how it
had been when I was born, everything in the world becoming both more vivid and more ordinary, and the black-and-
white world, the world of magic and shadows, disappearing
forever in my wake.

Now it's the scene where the men in blue jean coveralls are
wheeling props and sweeping the stage, carpenters shoulder-
ing boards, moving behind Gene Kelley as Don Lockwood
and Donald O'Connor as Cosmo. Cosmo is about to pull
his hat down over his forehead and sing, "Make 'em laugh!"
and hoof across the stage, pulling open a door only to be met
by a brick wall, careening up what appears to be a lengthy
marble-floored corridor but is in fact a painted backdrop.

Suddenly all the color drains from the room: not just from
the mottled sofa I'm lying on but also from the orange wall-
paper that looked so good on the shelf at Streeter's (and was
only $1.29 a roll), the chipped blue willow plate: everything's
black and silver now. I'm on a movie set, sitting in the director's chair. I'm grown up suddenly, eighteen or thirty-five.

Places, please!

Quiet on the set!

Speed! the soundman calls, and I point my index finger
at the camera, the clapper claps the board, and I see that
the movie we are making is called *Helen and Frida*. I slice
my finger quickly through the air and the camera rolls slowly forward toward Helen Keller and Frida Kahlo, who are
standing on a veranda with balustrades that appear to be
made of carved stone but are in fact made of plaster.

The part of Helen Keller isn't played by Patty Duke this
time; there's no *Miracle Worker* wild child to spunky rebel in

under one hundred minutes, no grainy film stock, none of that Alabama sun that bleaches out every soft shadow, leaving only harshness, glare. This time Helen is played by Jean Harlow.

Don't laugh: set pictures of the two of them side by side and you'll see that it's all there, the fair hair lying in looping curls against both faces, the same broad-cheeked bone structure. Imagine that Helen's eyebrows are plucked into a thin arch and penciled, lashes mascared top and bottom, lips cloisonnéd vermilion. Put Helen in pale peach mousseline de soie, hand her a white gardenia; bleach her hair from its original honey blond to platinum, like Harlow's was; recline her on a *Bombshell* chaise with a white swan gliding in front, a palm fan being waved overhead, while an ardent lover presses sweet nothings into her hand.

I play the part of Frida Kahlo.

It isn't so hard to imagine that the two of them might meet. They moved, after all, in not so different circles, fashionable and radical: Helen Keller meeting Charlie Chaplin and Mary Pickford, joining the Wobblies, writing in the *New York Times*, "I love the red flag . . . and if I could I should gladly march it past the offices of the *Times* and let all the reporters and photographers make the most of the spectacle"; Frida, friend of Henry Ford and Sergei Eisenstein, painting a hammer and sickle on her body cast, leaving her bed in 1954, a few weeks before her death, to march in her wheelchair with a babushka tied under her chin, protesting the overthrow of the Arbenz regime in Guatemala.

Of course, the years are all wrong, but that's the thing about the *Million Dollar Movie*: during Frank Sinatra Week, on Monday Frank would be young and handsome in *It*

Happened in Brooklyn, on Tuesday he'd have gray temples and crow's-feet, be older than my father, on Wednesday be even younger than he had been on Monday. You could pour the different decades in a bowl together and give them a single quick fold with the smooth edge of a spatula, the way my mother did when she made black-and-white marble cake from two Betty Crocker mixes. It would be 1912, and Big Bill Haywood would be waving the check Helen had sent over his head at a rally for the Little Falls strikers, and you, Frida, would be in the crowd, not as a five-year-old child, before the polio, before the bus accident, but as a grown woman, cheering along with the strikers. Half an inch away it would be August 31, 1932, and both of you would be standing on the roof of the Detroit Institute of the Arts, along with Diego, Frida looking up through smoked glass at the eclipse of the sun, Helen's face turned upward to feel the chill of night descending.

Let's get one thing straight right away. This isn't going to be one of those movies where they put their words into our mouths. This isn't *Magnificent Obsession*: blind Jane Wyman isn't going to blink back a tear when the doctors tell her they can't cure her after all, saying, "And I thought I was going to be able to get rid of these," gesturing with her ridiculous rhinestone-studded, cat's-eye dark glasses (and we think, "*Really*, Jane"); she's not going to tell Rock Hudson she can't marry him—"I won't have you pitied because of me. I love you too much," and "I could only be a burden"—and then disappear until the last scene when, as she lingers on the border between death and cure (the only two acceptable states), Rock saves her life and her sight and they live happily ever after. It's not going to be *A Patch of Blue*: when the sterling young Negro hands us the dark glasses and, in answer to our question, "But what are they for?" says, "Never mind, put them on," we're not going to grab them, hide our stone Medusa gaze, grateful for the magic that's made us a pretty girl. This isn't *Johnny Belinda*: we're not sweetly mute, surrounded by an aura of silence. No, in this movie the blind women have milky eyes that make the sighted uncomfortable. The deaf women drag metal against metal, oblivious to the jarring sound, make odd cries of delight at the sight of the ocean, squawk when we are angry.

So now the two female icons of disability have met: Helen, who is nothing but, who swells to fill up the category, sweet Helen with her drooping dresses covering drooping bosom, who is Blind and Deaf, her vocation; and Frida, who lifts her skirt to reveal the gaping, cunt-like wound on her leg, who rips her body open to reveal her back, a broken column, her back corset with its white canvas straps framing her beautiful breasts, her body stuck with nails; but she can't be Disabled, she's Sexual.

Here stands Frida, who this afternoon in the midst of a row with Diego cropped off her jet black hair ("Now see what you've made me do!"), and has schlepped herself to the ball in one of his suits. Nothing Dietrichish and coy about this drag: Diego won't get to parade his beautiful wife. Now she's snatched up Helen and walked with her out here onto the veranda.

In the other room drunken Diego lurches, his body rolling forward before his feet manage to shuffle themselves ahead on the marble floor, giving himself more than ever the appearance of being one of those children's toys, bottom-weighted with sand, that when punched roll back and then forward, an eternal red grin painted on its rubber face. His huge belly shakes with laughter, his laughter a gale that blows above the smoke curling up toward the distant gilded ceiling, gusting above the knots of men in tuxedos and women with marcelled hair, the black of their satin dresses setting off the glitter of their diamonds.

But the noises of the party, Diego's drunken roar, will be added later by the foley artists.

Helen's thirty-six. She's just come back from Montgomery. Her mother had dragged her down there after she and Peter Fagan took out a marriage license and the Boston papers got hold of the story. For so many years men had been telling her that she was beautiful, that they worshipped her, that when Peter declared himself in the parlor at Wrentham she had at first thought this was just more palaver about his pure love for her soul. But no, this was the real thing: carnal and thrilling and forbidden. How could you? her mother said. How people will laugh at you! The shame, the shame. Her mother whisked her off to Montgomery, Peter trailing after them. There her brother-in-law chased Peter off the porch with a good old southern shotgun. Helen's written her poem:

> *What earthly consolation is there for one like me*
> *Whom fate has denied a husband and the joy of*
>   *motherhood? . . .*
> *I shall have confidence as always,*
> *That my unfilled longings will be gloriously satisfied*
> *In a world where eyes never grow dim, nor ears dull.*

Poor Helen, waiting, waiting to get fucked in heaven.

Not Frida. She's so narcissistic. What a relief to Helen! None of those interrogations passing for conversation she usually has to endure (after the standard pile of praise is heaped upon her—I've read your book five, ten, twenty times, I've admired you ever since—come the questions: Do you mind if I ask you, Is everything black? Is Annie Sullivan *always* with you?): no, Frida launches right into the tale of Diego's betrayal. "Of course, I have my fun, too, but one doesn't want to have one's nose rubbed in the shit," she signs into Helen's hand.

Helen is delighted and shocked. In her circles Free Love is believed in, spoken of solemnly, dutifully. Her ardent young circle of socialists wants to do away with the sordid market-place of prostitution—bourgeois marriage—where women barter their hymens and throw in their souls to sweeten the deal; Helen has read Emma, she has read Isadora; she believes in a holy, golden monogamy, an unfettered eternal meeting of two souls-in-flesh. And here Frida speaks of the act so casually that Helen, like a timid schoolgirl, stutters, "You really? I mean, the both of you, you . . . ?"

Frida throws her magnificent head back and laughs. "Yes, really," Frida strokes gently into her hand. "He fucks other women and I fuck other men—and other women."

"F-U-C-K?" Helen asks. "What is this word?"

Frida explains it to her. "Now I've shocked you," Frida says.

"Yes, you have . . . I suppose it's your Latin nature . . ."

I'm not in the director's chair anymore. I'm sitting in the audience of the Castro Theater in San Francisco watching this unfold. I'm twenty-seven. When I was a kid I thought being grown up would be like living in the movies, that I'd be Rosalind Russell in *Sister Kenny*, riding a horse through the Australian outback, or that I'd dance every night in a sleek satin gown under paper palms at the Coconut Grove. Now I go out to the movies two, three, four times a week.

The film cuts from the two figures on the balcony to the night sky. It's Technicolor: pale gold stars against midnight blue. We're close to the equator now: there's the Southern Cross and the Clouds of Magellan, and you feel the press of the stars, the mocking closeness of the heavens as you can only feel it in the tropics. The veranda on which we are now standing is part of a colonial Spanish palace built in a clearing in a jungle that daily spreads its roots and tendrils closer, closer. A macaw perches atop a broken Mayan statue and calls, "I am queen / I am queen / I am queen." A few yards into the jungle a spider monkey shits on the face of a dead god.

Wait a minute. What's going on? Is that someone out in the lobby talking? But it's so loud—

Dolores del Rio strides into the film, shouting, "Latin nature! Who wrote this shit?" She's wearing black silk pants and a white linen blouse. She plants her fists on her hips and demands: "Huh? Who wrote this shit?"

I look to my left, my right, shrug, stand up in the audience, and say, "I guess I did."

"Latin nature! And a white woman? Playing Frida? I should be playing Frida."

"You?"

"Listen, honey." She's striding down the aisle toward me now. "I know I filmed that Hollywood crap. Six movies in one year: crook reformation romance, romantic Klondike melodrama, California romance, costume bedroom farce, passion in a jungle camp among chicle workers, romantic drama of the Russian revolution. I know David Selznick said, 'I don't care what story you use so long as we call it *Bird of Paradise* and Del Rio jumps into a flaming volcano at the finish.' They couldn't tell a Hawaiian from a Mexican from a lesbian. But I loved Frida and she loved me. She painted *What the Water Gave Me* for me. At the end of her life we were fighting, and she threatened to send me her amputated leg on a silver tray. If that's not love, I don't know what is—"

I'm still twenty-seven but now it's the year 2015. The Castro's still there, the organ still rises up out of the floor with the organist playing "San Francisco, open your Golden Gate." In the lobby, alongside the photos of the original opening of the Castro in 1927, are photos in black and white of lounging hustlers and leather queens, circa 1979, a photographic reproduction of the door of the women's room a few years later: "If they can send men to the moon, why don't they?" Underneath, in Braille, Spanish, and English: "In the 1960s, the development of the felt-tip pen, combined with a growing philosophy of personal expression, caused an explosion of graffiti . . . sadly unappreciated in its day, this portion of a bathroom stall, believed by many experts to have originated in the women's room right here at the Castro Theater, sold recently at Sotheby's for $5 million."

Of course, the Castro's now totally accessible, not just integrated wheelchair seating but every film captioned, an infrared listening device that interprets the action for blind people, over which now come the words: "As Dolores del Rio argues with the actress playing Frida, Helen Keller waits patiently—"

A woman in the audience stands up and shouts, "Patiently! What the fuck are you talking about, 'patiently'? You can't tell the difference between patience and powerlessness. She's being ignored." The stage is stormed by angry women, one of whom leaps into the screen and begins signing to Helen, "Dolores del Rio's just come out and—"

"Enough already!" someone in the audience shouts. "Can't we please just get on with the story!"

Now that Frida is played by Dolores, she's long haired again, wearing one of her white Tehuana skirts with a deep red shawl. She takes Helen's hand in hers, that hand that has been cradled by so many great men and great women.

"Latin nature?" Frida says and laughs. "I think perhaps it is rather your cold Yankee nature that causes your reaction." And before Helen can object to being called a Yankee, Frida says, "But enough about Diego . . ."

It's the hand that fascinates Frida, in its infinite, unpassive receptivity: she prattles on. When she makes the letters "z" and "j" in sign, she gets to stroke the shape of the letter into Helen's palm. She so likes the sensation that she keeps trying to work words with those letters in them into the conversation. The camera moves in close to Helen's hand as Frida says, "Here on the edge of the Yucatan jungle, one sometimes see jaguars, although never jackals. I understand jackals are sometimes seen in Zanzibar. I have never been there, nor have I been to Zagreb nor Japan nor the Zermatt, nor Java. I have seen the Oaxacan mountain Zempoaltepec. Once in a zoo in Zurich I saw a zebu and a zebra. Afterward, we sat in a small cafe and ate cherries jubilee and zabaglione, washed down with glasses of zinfandel. Or perhaps my memory is confused: perhaps that day we ate jam on zwieback crusts and drank a juniper tea, while an old Jew played a zither."

"Oh," says Helen.

Frida falls silent. Frida, you painted those endless self-portraits, but you always looked at yourself level, straight on, in full light. This is different: this time your face is tilted, played over by shadows. In all those self-portraits you are simultaneously artist and subject, lover and beloved, the bride of yourself. Now, here, in the movies, it's different: the camera stands in for the eye of the lover. But you're caught in the unforgiving blank stare of a blind woman.

And now we cut from that face to the face of Helen. Here I don't put in any soothing music, nothing low and sweet with violins, to make the audience more comfortable as the camera moves in for its close-up. You understand why early audiences were frightened by these looming heads. In all the movies with blind women in them—or, let's be real, sighted women playing the role of blind women—Jane Wyman and Irene Dunn in the different versions of *Magnificent Obsession*, Audrey Hepburn in *Wait until Dark*, we've never seen a blind woman shot this way before: never seen the camera come in and linger lovingly on her face the way it does here. We gaze at their faces only when bracketed by others' or in moments of terror when beautiful young blind women are being stalked. We've never seen before this frightening blank inward turning of passion, a face that has never seen itself in the mirror, that does not arrange itself for consumption.

Lack = inferiority? Try it right now. Finish reading this

paragraph and then close your eyes, push the flaps of your ears shut, and sit. Not just for a minute: give it five or ten. Not in that meditative state, designed to take you out of your mind, your body. Just the opposite. Feel the press of hand crossed over hand: without any distraction, you feel your body with the same distinctness as a lover's touch makes you feel yourself. You fold into yourself, you know the rhythm of your breathing, the beating of your heart, the odd independent twitch of a muscle: now in a shoulder, now in a thigh. Your cunt, in all its patient hunger.

We cut back to Frida in close-up. But now Helen's fingers enter the frame, travel across that face, stroking the downy mustache above Frida's upper lip, the fleshy nose, the thick-lobed ears.

Now it's Frida's turn to be shocked: shocked at the hunger of these hands, at the almost-feral sniff, at the freedom with which Helen blurs the line between knowing and needing.

"May I kiss you?" Helen asks.

"Yes," Frida says.

Helen's hands cup themselves around Frida's face.

I'm not at the Castro anymore. I'm back home on the foldout sofa in the slapped-together TV room, watching grainy images flickering on the tiny screen set in the wooden console. I'm nine years old again, used to Hays-office kisses, two mouths with teeth clenched, lips held rigid, pressing stonily against each other. I'm not ready for the way that Helen's tongue probes into Frida's mouth, the tongue that seems to be not so much interested in giving pleasure as in finding an answer in the emptiness of her mouth.

I shout, "Cut," but the two of them keep right on. Now we see Helen's face, her wide-open eyes that stare at nothing revealing a passion blank and insatiable, a void into which you could plunge and never, never, never touch bottom. Now she begins to make noises, animal mewlings and cries.

I will the screen to turn to snow, the sound to static. I do not want to watch this, hear this. My leg is in a thick plaster cast, inside of which scars are growing like mushrooms, thick and white in the dark damp. I think that I must be a lesbian, a word I have read once in a book, because I know I am not like the women on television, with their high heels and shapely calves and their firm asses swaying inside of satin dresses waiting, waiting for a man, nor am I like the women I know, the mothers with milky breasts, and what else can there be?

I look at the screen and they are merging into each other, Frida and Helen, the dark-haired and the light, the one who will be disabled and nothing more, the other who will be everything but. I can't yet imagine a world where these two might meet: the face that does not live under the reign of its own reflection with the face that has spent its life looking in the mirror; the woman who turns her rapt face up toward others and the woman who exhibits her scars as talismans; the one who is only, only and the one who is everything but. I will the screen to turn to snow.

Vincent

You all know the story of Vincent, the man with the scraggly
red hair and wild eyes, wearing the wrinkled linen suit, with
the battered straw hat sitting askew upon his head, Vincent
who at first seems destined to be a respectable, if slightly
eccentric, art dealer, like his burgher uncle. But at nine-
teen, Vincent is stranger than he was at eighteen, at twenty
stranger still. Vincent reads the Bible, the same Bible that his
father, Pastor Theodorus van Gogh, read to the assembled
congregation on Sunday, in his quavering voice that didn't
quite reach to the back of the small unheated church, to the
bored Dutch peasants for whom the Sunday visit in their
dark clothes to the dark church was but one more thing to
be endured in a life filled with things to be endured.

But when Vincent reads the Bible he hears the voice of
God who calls him to the wilderness to face him, the mad
holiness of scorned John the Baptist; when Vincent sees the
blackthorn hedges around the snow-covered fields, their

twisted bare black branches become characters upon the white paper of snow, reminding him of the pages of the gospel.

Vincent goes to preach in the coalfields of the Borinage, where to mortify his flesh he will sleep without a blanket on the coldest nights of the year, while the wind sails freely through the cracks in the rude hut. It is there that the children will chase him in the street, throwing rocks and calling, "He's mad! He's mad!" In the underground mines of the Borinage he will see the pit ponies, born in the darkness of the mines, dying without ever having seen the sun.

This is where the Hollywood version of his life begins, immediately after the opening credits, which give the great museums of the world, the Louvre and the Museum of Modern Art, top billing, above Kirk Douglas and Vincente Minelli even: without their help and that of private collectors across the world, this movie could not have been . . .

There's another film, now, a Robert Altman. This one opens not in Vincent's boyhood home nor in the coalfields of the Borinage but at Sotheby's. The climactic scene of Vincent's afterlife: the sale of *Sunflowers*: suited men in white gloves wheel out the painting: "5.5 million . . . 8 million, 500 thousand . . . 10 million . . ." The auctioneer's voice fades but is still in the background beneath a scene of filthy, tortured Vincent, pipe clenched in his teeth, lying on a filthy bed in a filthy hovel, rowing with his brother Theo. As Theo storms out, the auctioneer's voice rises: £21 million . . . £22 million, 500 thousand ." The gavel pounds. Judgment passed. (I suppose those of us who aren't philistines are meant to read this as irony.)

Vincent turns away from this evangelical path, writing to Theo: "I think that everything which is really good and beautiful—of inner moral, spiritual and sublime beauty in men and their works—comes from God, and that all which is bad and wrong in men and their works is not of God, and God does not approve of it. . . . To give you an example: someone loves Rembrandt, but seriously—that man will know there is a God, he will surely believe it."

Only this time around it's not 1885 but 1985. Theo doesn't live in Paris but in a co-op on West 53rd Street in New York. He's still an art dealer. He's just pulled off a real coup: selling an installation called *Empty Space*: one steps into a gallery, the walls are whitewashed, the artist's name appears in block letters on the wall—and there is nothing else. Theo, dressed in a slouchy teal silk shirt and wrinkled black linen pants, urges prospective buyers to simply allow themselves to experience *Empty Space*: the whiteness of the walls, the sounds of the city as they filter in through the silence. He may quote Rilke on the two subjects that the artist has, childhood and death, and how this installation starkly confronts us with our blank beginning, the abyss toward which we rush.

Theo's gone to see a therapist. She's helped him work through the thicket of guilt and envy, the legacies of that dysfunctional family, his neurotic need to support his manipulative, artist brother, the one named Vincent, the one who writes, "It is very urgent for me to have: 6 large tubes of chrome yellow, 1 citron, 6 large tubes malachite green, 10 zinc white," followed by another letter that asks, "Do you know what I have left today out of the money you sent this very day? Well, I have 6 francs. . . . So I really beg you to send me a louis, and that by return mail, please." The therapist shakes her head as Theo tells her that this Vincent was born a year to the day after the first son, also named Vincent, arrived in the world stillborn. Theo writes to his brother:

> Dear Vincent, I know that what I am going to say in this letter may well prove hard for you to hear. I have given this matter a great deal of thought. I realize that I have supported you financially as a way of not dealing with my own feelings of guilt and envy, that I have needed to feel superior to you. I have decided that I can no longer send you money as I have in the past.

So Vincent will never write those hundreds of letters to his brother filled with good elder-brother advice ("*Ora et labora*, let us do our daily work, whatever the hand finds to do, with all our strength and let us believe that God will give good gifts. . . . Courage, boy"); passages where his love of color melds with his feeling for the places he has traveled through, his love for his brother ("Before sunrise I had already heard the lark. When we were near the last station before London, the sun rose. The bank of gray clouds had disappeared and there was the sun, as simple and as grand as ever I saw it, a real Easter sun. The grass sparkled with dew and night frost. But I still prefer that gray hour when we parted"); biblical quotations ("God hath made us sorrowful yet always rejoicing"); and, later, his cool assessments of his mental state ("As far as I can judge, I am not properly speaking a madman") and the brotherhood of the asylum ("Though here there are some patients very seriously ill, the fear and horror of madness that I used to have has already lessened a great deal. And though here you continually hear terrible cries and howls like beasts in a menagerie, in spite of that people get to know each other very well and help each other when their attacks come on"). No, this time around Vincent does not fill up reams of paper with his firm, penciled script.

This time around, when Vincent gets this letter from Theo he crumples it up and throws it into the corner of his hotel room, a room cluttered with canvases and paints. *Trust in the Lord,* he tells himself. *He will provide.* He paints fifteen hours a day, devotes the few remaining hours to sleeping, eating instant oatmeal made with tap water as hot as he can get it out of the stingy faucets of the Metropolitan Hotel. (Vincent is the only resident who takes to heart the injunction intoned by the manager and repeated on signs Scotch-taped to the walls throughout the establishment: ABSOLUTELY NO COOKING IN THE ROOMS, while the hallways are thick with the smells of curries and boiled cabbages and hamburger grease.)

But then, when the landlord changes the lock on Vincent's room, demanding the three weeks' back rent, adding, "And don't think I'm going to store that junk of yours for long!" Vincent sets out to find a job. He scavenges newspapers from trashcans and looks through the classifieds; he walks from McDonald's to Wendy's to Burger King, dutifully filling out applications. PAST EMPLOYMENT HISTORY: art dealer, minister. REASON FOR LEAVING: heard the call of God, loss of faith. Poor, mad Vincent! For two weeks he tramps the streets in the linen suit that shrunk and was thus passed down to him from Theo, so short that it shows a gap of pasty flesh between the top of his sock and the cuff of his pants, a porkpie hat set atop his wild flame of hair.

Finally he goes to Social Security to apply for benefits. He takes a number (32), like in a deli. Sitting next to him in an identical molded plastic orange chair is a boy with a bright red seizure helmet; across from them a retiree. Hours pass. Finally a voice mumbles his number.

"Name?" says the worker by way of greeting, following that with "Address?" Vincent gives the address of Our Place, a Bowery social service agency that collects his mail for him. "Date of birth?"

"Have you ever been diagnosed as having a psychiatric impairment?"

"No. But the children chase me in the street and throw stones at me and call 'He's mad! He's mad!'"

The intake worker: a man with a shaggy bowl cut like the Beatles had in 1964, a man who wears a too-large pair of glasses that slide down his nose, a "C" student.

"The regulations of Social Security," he says, with his eyes fixed on a point on the distant wall, "provide for benefits to those who can be shown, by objective tests and measurements," pushing his glasses with his forefinger back up the bridge of his nose, "to have an impairment, whether mental, emotional or physical, which prevents them from engaging in employment."

"Oh," says Vincent, "I can work. I paint fifteen hours a day. It's just that everyone thinks I'm mad."

"Objective tests and measurements," the intake worker repeats, backing thirty seconds into his speech. The wheels of Social Security grind slowly, and they grind exceedingly small. Vincent must wait, and wait and wait. The landlord burns his canvases, throws away his paints. Poor, mad, hungry Vincent walks the streets of New York. My art is what I see, Vincent tells himself. My art is an ever-changing canvas I paint in my head.

Finally a notice arrives at Our Place. "An appointment has been scheduled for you."

Vincent enters the psychiatrist's office. The shrink is mid-forties, a smooth dome pate, not very successful, and so has ended up taking these cases. Mostly he weeds out the fakers, the ones whose notions of craziness have been formed by TV, and tell him of arms reaching out of the walls, monsters trailing up the stairs, vivid hallucinations; he winnows them apart from the more steady parade of those quagmired in misery.

"Mr. Van Go."

"Van Gogh," Vincent corrects him.

"Van Goff."

"Just call me Vincent."

"Mr. Vincent. Have a seat."

Irritable, the shrink notes; that and the fact that this Mr. Vincent has chosen the seat closest to him.

This is not a standard psychiatric first encounter. There is no silence as an opening gambit, no "What brings you here today?" no patient wait for the patient to begin. Instead the doctor, yellow legal pad on his lap, writes briskly: name; address; with whom do you live? Do you work? No? Have you ever worked? Parents living? Sisters and brothers? Names; ages; what do they do? Glancing at his watch, he sees it's time to move on to: Ever hear voices? Have mood swings?

Vincent does not dissemble. He tells the bored shrink everything. Yes, he hears the voice of God. It speaks to him sometimes in the night; it speaks to him through the flowers and trees, the blades of grass pushing their way up through the Manhattan sidewalks. He tells the shrink that he read

Thomas à Kempis's *Imitation of Christ* and tried to live the life of a true Christian, taking seriously the biblical injunction "Take all you have and give it to the poor," doling out his bedclothes, his food, his clothing.

Poor self-esteem, the shrink notes.

Vincent's chair will hardly contain him. He waves his arms so wildly that the doctor moves objects back on his desk: the vase holding the dried flower arrangement, his black lamp. Several times the shrink murmurs, "Calm yourself, Mr. Vincent," and "We need to move on, Mr. Vincent."

At the end of the session Vincent is dismissed. "That's all?" he asks. He had spoken to this man with such rare honesty, it seemed their souls had touched: the doctor had murmured, "Yes, tell me more" as Vincent told him about the face of God glowing through the sunflower.

That night as he drives home on the Long Island Expressway, the doctor dictates a letter to the Social Security Administration. In bumper-to-bumper traffic, the drivers around him bopping about in their bucket seats to the songs blasting out of their car radios or with blank, unfocused stares, the doctor speaks into the voice-activated mike: "On September 21, 1985, Mr. Vincent—Estelle, get the information, Social Security number and everything from the notes, which I'm attaching . . ." Vincent has dropped himself neatly into the category of schizo-affective disorder: the religious mania and the sheer joy, the inappropriate ecstasy, that the color yellow evokes in him.

The next morning Estelle types the letter; by that afternoon it has been signed, folded, placed in an envelope, stamped, and mailed.

Yet Vincent hears nothing from the Social Security Administration.

What do we imagine happened to that letter? That it traveled promptly through the mails to Washington DC, and there was delivered to a mausoleum-like building of granite? That within that building a woman sits alone at a battered wooden desk, a battered wooden desk with a few devices upon it: an elaborate rack holding rubber stamps, a stamp pad, a letter opener, and a stapler? That in the top drawer of this desk sit identical purple-inked stamp pads, shrink-wrapped in clear plastic; that the bottom two drawers are filled full with neat stacks of boxes of five thousand staples each? That behind her is a mountain range of letters—letters from doctors, petitions from rejected applicants, requests for clarification from muddled recipients?

She swivels slowly in her wooden chair and extracts a single letter from one mountain. Her eyes travel slowly over the address. At first one thinks of the gaze with which a letter from a lover is studied: the eyes caress the handwriting; one stares at the stamp: if it's a commemorative, you imagine that she went to the post office, chose carefully, the one you would appreciate most. If it's a standard American flag you figure that in her hurry to get it off to you, she rummaged in a desk drawer, grabbed the first thing that came to hand.

But this woman isn't alive with desire. With a slack jaw, a dull gaze, she makes sure that the envelope is properly addressed: if the zip code is wrong, she leans slowly forward, slowly turns the metal rack of rubber stamps in front of her until she finds the one that says, "Incorrect Zip Code/Return to Sender." If the address is off by so much as a single digit, it too is sent back. If all is in order, with practiced slowness she lifts the letter opener, inserts it into the ungummed corner, slowly, slowly tears the envelope open, lifts the letter out, unfolds it, smoothes out the creases; lifts the largest of her rubber stamps, her very favorite, with its elaborate rubber loops of numbers, its cogs and arrows, presses the stamp firmly against the purple ink pad, then finally against the letter, rocking it ever so slowly back and forth: "Rec'd ssa, 10:00 a.m., September 24, 1985." Every hour a buzzer rings, and she pushes the time arrow ahead an hour. At 10:00 and again at 2:00, a skinny young man wheels in great baskets of mail to add to the mountain behind her.

Vincent, poor Vincent, wanders the streets of the city. He has not eaten for days. The first day or so without food, hunger makes you peevish, self-pitying. You notice how much of the world is given over to eating: two or three storefronts out of every block are restaurants: diners sit in windows, waiting patiently at their white-topped tables with a basket of French bread set in front of them from which they occasionally tear a piece, munching slowly, thoughtlessly (what you wouldn't do, Vincent, for a taste of that bread!); they eat pastrami sandwiches and pizzas, glistening with fat, dripping mustard or globs of tomato sauce onto black beards, blouses; mom-and-pop stores display their cans of fava beans and *frijoles negros*, their potato chips (Cajun, sour cream and onion, bleu cheese), Fritos, Cheetos, candy racks holding Baby Ruths, Oh Henry's!, Fifth Avenues, Butterfingers, Lifesavers; women emerge from grocery stores, pushing carts loaded with children and paper or plastic sacks heavy with frozen corn, spinach, peas, broccoli; fresh oranges, apples, cucumbers, celery; tins of tuna, cans of condensed milk; steaks, tofu; boneless, skinless chicken breasts. Thin women with good cheekbones sashay from take-out emporiums with white containers; signs blink EAT, EAT, EAT. The world seems to be organized around a single principle: the shoving of food into a great maw, outside of which you stand, gaunt, pale, with a stomach that twists and cramps with unsated desire.

In the midst of your frantic yearning, you know—the knowledge a dim reality—that in a day or two this hunger will cease to bedevil you; it will be replaced by a feeling of pure, transcendent calm. The pangs of hunger will burn themselves out, burn away all longing. In another twenty-four hours you will walk through the canyons of New York, beaming benevolently at all the rushing yups, the dawdling homeless, the hue and cry. You will have slept the previous night under a blanket of light from the moon, will have awakened this morning in Central Park, the birds weaving a canopy of song over your head, trilling, "Vincent, Vincent, Vincent." You will be happy.

Impossible, however, to live for too long in that holy state without food. On your wax and feather wings of hunger you know you are soaring too close to the sun: your happiness becomes frantic, high-pitched, a few steps away from madness. So you scavenge garbage cans for returnable bottles, panhandle, look for the odd penny or dime lying on the street. You go to a McDonald's and buy a small milk, a single hamburger, which, like a drug, is both salvation and damnation, a holy paradox. You are saved from the ecstatic state that can only end in death but delivered again into that cycle of need and want, the reawakening of the flesh.

And the reawakening of despair. When you are not eating the food you imagine is the stuff of dreams: home-baked bread dripping with sweet creamery butter, salads of romaine lettuce dressed with extra virgin olive oil and tarragon vinegar, salmon so delicate it dissolves in your mouth; a cheddar that your grandfather unwrapped from a cheesecloth and granted you a sliver of one Christmas Eve. And then there is the reality of the cloying milk and the hamburger that tastes of metal and decay. And the reaction of an empty stomach to food, which forces you to rush down an alley, pull down your pants, and allow the shit to hiss and roil out of you.

Meanwhile, she sits, the mountain of letters growing ever taller behind her, and with studied lassitude opens an envelope, pulls out the letter, stamps it with her "Rec'd" stamp, staples the envelope onto the back of the letter, rolls the letter and inserts it into a pneumatic tube, which carries it down. Down to a vast underground nest of bureaucrats, who, like the pit ponies of the Borinage, have never seen the light of day. They are born, mate, reproduce, and die in this fluorescent-lit hell. Only through dim recounting do they have any knowledge of the world above: that day gives way to starry night, that the Social Security numbers they give out and process are attached to living human beings. They do not know that the struggles for the twelve- and then the ten-, the eight-hour day have been won. Pale as white worms, they labor fourteen hours a day, wearing old-fashioned green eyeshades and creosote cuffs. They sleep next to their desks on folding cots, covered with Civil War–era army surplus scratchy wool blankets. They mate quickly, furtively in cubicles and broom closets, give shameful birth in stalls of the women's room. The new forms (SSA-L8170-U3; SSA-561-U2) appear mysteriously in the supply room; they take comfort in the notations in the upper-right-hand corners—"Form approved OMB"; religiously follow the directives, "Exhaust existing supplies of SSA-L8710-U2" or "Destroy prior editions," which they do in rituals held around the paper shredder. These are directives from their God, OMB whose face they cannot imagine, whose name they are forbidden to speak.

Vincent falls in love with a prostitute. Even in the Robert Altman version, where we see Sien crouching over the chamber pot to piss, even in that raw and gritty film, she's not ugly. But I've seen Vincent's drawings of Sien. She was. Her breasts weren't symmetrical and they lay in flat folds against her chest. Her face was wan. I know Sien. I pass her every day in Detroit's Cass Corridor, she sits in the booth next to me at Coney King, I see her in Parker's buying a single beer and a half liter of Pepsi. On a rich woman her fine features, the skin tight against jutting cheekbones, would look beautiful or at least dramatic, but on her poverty, exhaustion, bitterness leave her looking haggard, too thin, as she lurches forward on spiked heels.

Poor Vincent: you shocked your uncle Cor by telling him that you loved ugly women, that you would rather be with someone whose pain and past were written on her face. But even Altman won't allow an ugly woman to appear on film.

Vincent, starving Vincent, refuses to allow Sien to give him any of the money she gets from ADC. So he goes down to General Assistance. Literally: the GA offices are in the basement of the City/County Welfare Building, the building with the marble facade and the white marble figures with perfectly muscled bodies that embody justice, civic duty, freedom, down into the linoleum-paved hallways, half lit by flickering fluorescent lights. Nearly two hundred of them, men (a few women), most, but not all, of whom have bathed within the past week, wait. Some scratch, some rock slowly in their seats, some keep up a steady flow of curses. Vincent waits and waits and waits; at the end of the day he is given a number and told to come back again; the next day he waits, and the day after that is given $160 a month, found eligible for food stamps, given a Transit Pass.

He sells his food stamps for 65¢ on the dollar, stands at a freeway entrance holding a sign that reads, "Will Work for Food," although who would dream of asking this man to do odd jobs at her home, what restaurant owner would offer him work busing tables? But cars do stop, offering folded dollars, spare change. With the money he scrounges, Vincent buys a canvas, paints.

Vincent is going to paint light.

But before he can paint light he must paint darkness. He must paint the picture of the five homeless people in the abandoned building, four men and one woman, a flashlight dangling from a rope tied to a lighting fixture above them casts deep shadows on their faces, as they share a meal of two orders of large fries and Chicken McNuggets, the puny light turning the white paper gray. He must paint the picture of the Haitian refugees working in the dusk, not turning on their lights, doing illegal homework in their one-room apartment. He must paint the still life of the three pairs of shoes that he pulled from trashcans and dumpsters; he must paint the skull against black holding a burning cigarette in its teeth.

While Vincent yearns toward the light, in Washington DC a Programmer descends into the dark bowels of the Social

Security Administration. Wiry-haired, wiry, with an astonishingly large Adam's apple that jounces up and down as he speaks, speaks the language which they, the underground beings, recognize as English, although its meaning is incomprehensible to them: "swizzling between multiple files," "I've hacked lisp machines," "the code that you snarf from the net," "the domain of munging text." He is here to devise a vast Network that will link this mother-office to the offices on the surface, to take this system where clerks still scratch with quill pens and rolled documents are pulled from pneumatic tubes and bring it—not just online but into the greatest mainframe humanity has ever known.

At first the Programmer sends up three times a day for double espresso, which arrives in ecologically correct paper cups with not quite so ecologically correct plastic covers. He downs one at 10:00 a.m., one at noon, and the third at 3:00 in the afternoon. Each morning he descends in the elevator and each evening ascends.

He is happy, if such a mundane word can be applied to a man who mastered differential equations at the age of seven, who can recite the entire dialogue of every episode of *The Prisoner*. He daydreams of installing a terminal in every maternity ward and birth center. Infants assigned Social Security numbers at birth, entered along with their weight, height, sex, and Apgar scores! Terminals in every morgue and funeral parlor, to close the files of the dead!

He imagines himself as Colonel Kilgore in *Apocalypse Now* (he has seen it thirty-seven times, twelve at the movies and twenty-five times on video). He inwardly crows, "I love the smell of napalm in the morning!" as he strides through the sub-sub-subbasement, past the GS 2s and 3s whom he leaves

trembling in his wake, although they see in his unnatural-
ly long stride, the way he pumps his arms in front of him,
the off-gait of the maniac, declaiming to his assistant, "The
question of whether C or Lisp or Emacs Lisp or ML or Shell
or any of the little languages is the appropriate method to
attack a problem is a religious one . . . I want tools that work
together, not one program that generates VSAM fixed-length
eighty-byte record files and can't play with another, can read
only other format files. I want to be able to glue those programs easily and trivially reap the benefits of coarse-grain
parallelism."

At first he dutifully clocks in, 9:00 to 5:00: no work-ob-
sessed Yuppie he; he knows where his real life lies: in front of
the television he jerry-rigged himself with the remote control
feature that enables him with a simple motion of his thumb
to make the screen go fuzzy, the browns red, the blues ma-
genta, turning back episodes of *Dobie Gillis* and *The Aveng-
ers* into expressionist art. His real life lies with his elaborate
computer game in which he casts as villains anyone who has
ever wronged him: his third-grade teacher, Mrs. Kaplan; his
older brother who lives in the Bay Area and disputes arcane
points of Trotskyist doctrine with his coreligionists; the gang
of kids who took one look at him on a Cambridge street five
years ago and beat him senseless: all stand in the way of the
elusive, nameless Maiden, a woman he once saw in a white
dress, backlit by a porch light, coming down the steps of
a California bungalow whom he has loved devotedly ever
since.

But one evening the Programmer looks up at the clock,
realizes that time has flown by: it is 7:30: he has missed the
Dr. Who rerun on Channel 42. He slams his fists on the

computer keyboard, shouts, "Fuck! Fuck! Fuck-Fuck-Fuck-Fuck," but then goes back to work.

Before long he has almost become one of them. No longer do the espressos arrive from above at three-hour intervals: instead his assistant finds that his duties have devolved to being merely a cappuccino runner. He ascends to the above and fetches double lattes, caffè macchiatos, triple mochas for the Programmer, coming back trembling at what he has seen: the brilliant pulsing yellow globe of the sun, the flickering green leaves, the stark white marble and granite buildings of the Capitol, the wild buckets of flowers set out for sale next to the Metro station. He returns dizzy, almost nauseous with the riot of color, afraid to speak of it to those who live underground, pale as blank slugs in their murky world of slate, smudged brown, mole.

At 3:00 one morning the exhausted Programmer, who has an 8:00 a.m. meeting, decides it isn't worth going home to sleep, and so sets up a cot next to his terminal. As he pulls the scratchy wool blanket, redolent with a century's worth of odors, up to his chin, he little imagines how few times he will again see the sun. The next evening he will leave after 9:00 and fall asleep in front of the vid running episode number 15 of *The Brady Bunch* (he displays his porn proudly and keeps his *Brady Bunch* tape under his socks in a bureau drawer). Then for four more weeks he will not even surface again.

Meanwhile he has had installed a La Pavoni, the queen of espresso machines, at which his assistant now toils, making him endless cups of brackish espresso. He has almost ceased to eat.

The clerks with whom he must interface stare at him slack

jawed, refuse to comprehend his frenetic speech. And endless glitches appear in the circuitry. They think they've found the root of the problem when they discover that the circuit boards are being deliberately mis-soldered, electrical connections skewed by the workers of Multinational Memory's On Wok Long Factory No. 3: unionization efforts there having been stymied by repressive legislation and random firings, the workers have formed the Rosa Luxembourg–King Lud anarcho-syndicalist collective with the slogan "The Barricades are in the Circuit Boards." But even when the circuit boards are repaired and Legal has filed a multibillion-dollar lawsuit against Multinational Memory that promises, in its scope and complexity, to take years if not decades to wend its way through the court system—

But we have almost forgotten poor Vincent! Where is he? The last time we saw him he was standing at a freeway entrance holding his sign. We return to that same freeway entrance, but he is not there: we search the city, checking out each of those unshaven, unwashed men holding signs, the men huddled around burning barrels, hanging on street corners outside shelters and service providers and liquor stores. He's nowhere. Has he died in some back alley? Left Manhattan on foot, walking across the Brooklyn Bridge, trudging through Flatbush and Prospect Park, heading out to find the Long Island that Whitman wrote about?

But no, Vincent has not left the city, not gone into the countryside to paint light: he's sleeping some nights in a Bowery flophouse, sometimes sleeping days and walking the streets all the dangerous night long. Weekly he treks to Our Place, where the volunteer behind the desk flips through the vs and says. "Nothing. Sorry." Vincent turns and walks away, then turns back. "Perhaps it was—under G?" he ventures.

She sighs, rifles the letters filed under G and says, with satisfaction, "No."

Once there is something for him, but when the letter is handed to him Vincent is dismayed to see that it is merely from his brother Theo: a card of a Seurat print, "Think of you so often and hope that you are well."

But then, at last, one day it is there: when Vincent goes into Our Place and stutters to the woman at the front of the line: "Van Gogh, it's two words, V-A-N and then G-O-G-H, and so sometimes I get filed under V and other times under G . . . ," he is handed an official letter. It would take the talents of one of the great romantic poets to describe the throbbing of Vincent's heart inside his pale chest, the rush of delighted color flooding his cheeks. With trembling, trembling hands he tears open the envelope. Without salutation the letter begins: "We are increasing your benefit amount" and then goes on to say, "We cannot pay you any benefit at this time." Vincent reads these words over and over again. He can make no sense of them. He meditates on this bureaucratic koan.

Vincent does not know that the first part of the Network has at last gone online and begun to generate these letters. Ten years previously a consulting firm (which actually consisted of a woman with a master's degree in educational psych and a part-time secretary) landed a multimillion-dollar contract to draft these epistles, mandated by an act designed to simplify the baroque language of the Bureaucracy, as convoluted as medieval Latin, into a Basic English understandable by over 95 percent of the U.S. population. So now instead of Byzantine incomprehensibility we have a clean Zen paradox: "We are increasing your benefit amount . . . we cannot pay you any benefit at this time."

And that letter from the good doctor that officially certifies Vincent as mad? Where has that gone? Thank God we are the Godlike narrator of this piece, that we have the power to peer into the great mountain of letters and immediately find Vincent's, that we do not have to paw through the tens of thousands of pieces beneath which it is buried: pleas from former miners with brown lung, desperate letters from mothers of chronically ill children, Xeroxed medical records still awaiting their official purple "Rec'd" stamps. There it is, about three feet down, waiting, waiting still.

But the Programmer is hard at work. Geeked on espresso, his fingers roil over the keyboard as his plans for the Network become ever greater: now it will be linked into banking system computers, spying on recipients to ensure that they are not collecting unreported interest on their checking accounts, depositing unpedigreed sums of cash, into the computers of every college and university; it will be modemed into links between doctors' offices and medical labs, insurance companies, it will pick up credit card transactions, driving records, so that when an applicant shows up at an office of the Bureaucracy, the tapping in of her Social Security number will produce a complete educational, medical, social, and psychological profile.

Alas, the poor Programmer! Unbeknownst to him, a tumor is growing in his brain, fed by the electromagnetic fields that pulse from his computer; his story, like the story of Vincent, is tragic. He will not live to see the Network go online.

"Caffè macchiato," he calls out to his assistant. "Make it a triple." He, who once checked his e-mail every waking hour, has become so obsessed with the Network that sheaves of messages pile up: from hackers in Australia and Azerbaijan, from his college roommate who is trying to get him to come to a celebration of Nikolai Tesla's 129th birthday. The message that follows: "All work and no play make Jack a dull boy," scrolls endlessly down the screen.

Vincent, who has not been able to scrounge any more money for canvas or paint, a street-corner crazy, perches himself on a broken-down chair he has found in an alley and, palette-less, canvas-less, begins to paint in the air. He paints the *Cafe Terrace at Night*, the yellow light spilling out of the bar, the night-blue sky above, alive with the dotted streetlights that glow like fireflies. Holding an imaginary brush in his hand, he leans forward to his imaginary canvas, swiftly painting the black, yellow, orange, and blue streaks that make the sidewalk. How thickly he would lay on the texture of the zinc white that costs $8.58 a tube.

Poor, mad Vincent: he sits in the public library and stares, stares at the man sitting opposite him, imagining how he would paint him: exaggerating the fairness of the hair with oranges, chromes, even pale citron yellows. Behind the head he would paint infinity, a plain background of the richest, intensest blue that he could contrive: a mysterious effect, so the face would be like a star in the depths of an azure sky. The face has something more to say to him: he stares and stares, until the man slams the book he is reading shut, gets up, and moves to another table.

Poor, mad Vincent: his imaginary paint never speaks back

to him the way real paint does. It never refuses to do his bidding, surprises him. Vincent, in real life, pardon the expression, you dipped your fingers into the paint and made the curving petals of the sunflowers with your thumb. Later on, Vincent, when you were going mad, you drank turpentine, tasted Prussian blue paint, profane Communion.

Leaning in a doorway, his shopping cart filled with aluminum cans, Japanese prints torn from art books in the library, sharing his bottle of Midnight Express with a companion he has just met, a black man who tells Vincent that whites are the devil, marked by those eerie blue eyes of theirs. "Hiroshima," the man ticks off, "slavery," taking a swig, "concentration camps . . ." Vincent, who believes so easily, believes. He remembers that Christ said, "If a man hate not his life, he cannot be my disciple," and, full of self-hatred, stares at his pasty white flesh with its mottled blues and yellows and pinks. He stares at his companion: missing half his teeth, his face covered with odd bumps, his fingernails thick and yellowed, more like the hooves of cattle than the smooth, shaped nails of that other race, the rich. Together the two men dream aloud of the sun-drenched skies of Martinique, Java, Africa. There they will know the truth: that the only real infidels are those who don't believe in the sun.

There's a high yellow note Vincent has to attain to do his best work: to get there he has to be pretty keyed up, on endless coffee, loaves of Wonder Bread, and cheap, cheap wine. But on it he will paint the colors beneath the stark flesh-colors called black and white: the orange and yellow and green hues of his own skin, the same tones that underlie his companion's skin, to bring together for a moment in color what history has rent apart.

You all know how this story ends: Vincent dies. In the Hollywood version, he is at his easel painting *Crows over the Wheat Field*, a shrink's dream of a painting made by someone with bipolar disorder: the yellow fields of joyous wheat, malevolent skies brooding above, and the crows—the only living thing in the painting, the crows—carrying darkness down into the light. Kirk Douglas's face expresses agony, torment, and he pulls out the revolver. The camera cuts discreetly away to a farmer passing in a wooden wagon and we hear the shot.

But this time it isn't in Hollywood and it isn't in Auvers. At the very moment when Vincent fires the shot, at that exact moment, the white woman behind the wooden desk at last reaches the letter from Vincent's doctor and stamps it: "Rec'd., July 27, 1990, 11:00 a.m."

The Artist and the Dwarf

The dwarf's name was Mari Barbola. She glares out from the lower-right-hand corner of Velázquez's *Las meninas*, a painting that hangs in a darkened room of its own in Madrid's Prado, above a marble plaque reading *La obra culminante del arte universal*: the culminating work of universal art.

It is a curious painting: the seemingly casual arrangement of the figures, the vast looming darkness that takes up a good two-thirds of the canvas give it the effect of a snapshot, somehow overexposed at the bottom and underexposed above, almost as if a tourist had taken a wrong turn in the halls of the Alcazar and found herself in a corridor leading back three hundred–odd years, the rubber soles of her Adidas squeaking against the marble tiles of the palace floor, the snap of her gum echoing in the sepulchral halls, until, turning a corner, she suddenly caught a glimpse of the royal assembly and lifted her Kodak to snap this picture where no one, save Velázquez, who sneers out at her with a courtier's contempt for a barbarian, is aware of her presence: catching this canvas before the figures on it dissolve back into the air of time.

Mari Barbola is scarcely taller than the five-year-old white-white Infanta Margarita, the center of the painting, the child of an Austrian mother and a Hapsburg father, the two pale monarchs who rule over this dark-eyed, dark-haired people, who in turn rule over others with darker eyes and darker hair. Mari Barbola stares out of the canvas, her doughy face defiant: she is the only one of nonroyal blood in the painting who does not bend, kneel, lean. She stands upright. Unlike the dwarf next to her, his slipper-clad foot resting on the back of a docile Alsatian, she is no perfect miniature. As big around as she is tall, the critics who write in centuries to come will cavalierly describe her as "ugly." But we know who makes the rules: who blesses the vapid, worm-white *infanta* with the word "beautiful," decides that the blond halo of hair surrounding her face is to die for.

Barbola was brought to Madrid from Germany, having been sold by her parents to a passing noble who offered them ten astonishing pieces of silver (they could scarcely suppress their glee: she had accompanied them to market not to be sold but to watch over the stall as they went about their business), then given by this viscount as a gift to a Spanish noble, and finally passed up to the king.

And so she found herself, on the 17th day of September 1632, conveyed into Madrid in the back of a cart, the city where Philip IV's grandfather had settled the itinerant Spanish court, which previously had proceeded in an sluggish imperial round from Toledo to Valladolid to Burgos—Madrid, which had been a miserable town on a barren Castilian plain, battered by hot winds in the summer and cold winds in the winter. Oh, foolish, foolish Philip! Why did you fix your court here, in the dead center of Spain, far from the ports where your ships set sail to the distant dominions that are your wealth? Why did you build the great carved Segovia gate, the ornate entryway into this crude boomtown of muddy streets and slapped-together shacks and open sewers? With all those fey, turreted castles of Spain, why do you chose to lock yourself up here in this squat, thick-walled, narrow-windowed fortress, the Alcazar?

But to Mari Barbola, a daughter of the Bavarian peasantry who had grown up in a one-room lumber hut, with pigs and a donkey and a cow (the years her family was lucky enough to have a cow) rooting and braying and lowing about her, and then had spent a year or two in a dark cranny of the viscount's upper rooms, this Madrid with its rouge-cheeked ladies with their ruff collars of linen spun so fine it is translucent, then locked into stiff waves (wheat going for starch while the uprooted peasants wander the countryside eating herbs and roots), those collars that seem to capture movement, the gem-encrusted farthingales that catch light and fling it laughingly back, both forbidden by the endlessly contravened sumptuary laws, this Madrid seemed an incandescent city.

Oh, foolish, foolish race of Philips! In *Las meninas*, Philip IV, alongside his second queen, is reflected dimly in a distant mirror. In the earlier portraits Velázquez painted of him, Philip is dressed in black tights that do as much as they can to disguise his knobby knees; a pasty-faced, liver-lipped youth attempts a regal pose in *Philip IV in Armor*, but with his peach fuzz mustache and frightened eyes, it is not hard to imagine him hanging out at the mall, a Marlboro dangling from his lips, willing to be the butt of his companions' jokes for the privilege of being near them; his queen, Mariana of Austria, is a sullen flat-chested half-child, overwhelmed by her hoop skirts of woven gold and silver and pearls; her hair fixed into an elaborate starched coif that echoes the shape of the flying buttresses of her skirts.

Poor you! Poor Philip! lost in the mist of his titles: His Most Catholic Majesty, King of the Spains, Old and New, King of the Goths, of Austria, of Lusitania, of Celtiberia, of Cantabria, of Italy, of Flanders, the Planet King, King of Castile and Aragon, of the two Sicilies, Jerusalem, Portugal, the Canary Islands, of the East and West Indies, Archduke and Phoenix of the Fragrant Remains of the House of Austria, king over the future realm of the LA freeways, Aspen, John Wayne Airport, Acapulco, the beachfront condos in Puerto Vallarta, the tin mines of Bolivia, the street corners all across Latin America where the Chiclet vendors sell their wares, Caracas, Buenos Aires, etc., ruler of Picardy, Luxembourg, the Philippines; King of Slaves and Slavers and Torturers, Defender and Zealous Protector of the Blessed Virgin's Immaculate Conception, Duke of Brabant, Duke of Milan, Count of Flanders, Count of Tyrol, Count of Barcelona, Monarch of Shadows.

But although Philip is king, Mariana of Austria is not yet queen the day that Mari Barbola arrives in Madrid: someone else fills that role, an Isabella, this one of Bourbon, who, like her successor, gives birth to robust girls and sickly boys. It is to one of these frail, pale *infantes*, Baltasar Carlos, that Mari Barbola becomes companion.

I know what you expect of her: that she'll either be a dull

stone before whom the swirling waters of palace intrigue part or she'll be a mini-Rasputin who spends her first years at court staring dully and accumulating a storehouse of valuable gossip, which she'll later unleash to good use, finding herself petted and curried and hated. But she's neither: she figures out what she needs to know, but she isn't vicious; she's as devious and placid as you or I. She eats the leftovers from the royal table: she's happy.

Not that life at the court is any smooth round of pleasures. The pale and sickly prince dies, to be replaced by another pale prince who in turn, etc., until his mother, his noble, petted mother, who is dressed in gold and lace and swathed in titles and humped like a brood mare—weakened from the unceasing rounds of pregnancies and births, fades, falls ill, and, although the holy corpse of St. Isidore the Husbandman and a fragment of the True Cross are brought to her bedside, dies. How often Mari Barbola finds herself dressed in black mourning and shuffling off to the Convent of the Discalced Carmelites or to the mausoleum of a palace called El Escorial, the slag heap, to attend another internment or say yet another Mass for the repose of a royal soul.

Sometimes the gloomy round is broken by an auto-da-fé. The best are held in the Plaza Mayor: once Mari even got to sit with the king and queen and the infante (was it Baltasar Carlos or was he dead by then? Maybe it was one of the infantas; she can't quite remember) in their balcony draped with velvet of oxblood red held back by swags made of pure gold. The ceremony must begin at night, because the processional from the Convent of Doña Maria de Aragon, which bears the great green cross, is followed by great gangs of priests bearing waxen tapers, torchbearers, and faggot bearers, yes, fire must be brought from every single monastery and nunnery in Madrid, and—well, you can't imagine the torchlight procession of the Nazi Youth in *Triumph of the Will* happening in broad daylight, can you? But of course, the actual burning of the heretics couldn't happen in the dark, because nobody would be able to see a thing. No, so there has to be a solemn, nightlong vigil, the flames kept alive with great ceremony.

I wish that she had shuddered, my Mari, sneered (sure, sure, and then the portrait of Christ wept tears of blood, yeah, uh-huh), but she didn't. While the queen blushes red as the charge is read about unnatural acts with the Devil right there in the lap of the Holy Mother church, Mari leans forward, full of lascivious disgust. She doesn't avert her eyes for a single moment as each monastery adds its touch of flame to the bonfire.

The next morning the Jews are brought out. They pretended to have converted, but really in their hearts they never bought that God's seed entered the womb of Mary through her ear or that four days dead, Lazarus draped his grave clothes over his arm and trotted happily out of his tomb. After five years of imprisonment and torture, they have confessed it all: yes, just as the Inquisition was informed, they met secretly and tortured a picture of Christ, who came alive and gently, mournfully rebuked them for this sin, but no, they did not listen. What did they do then? Why, then they all went out and sneaked into churches, stole the consecrated Host and wolfed it down like naughty boys at the cookie jar, pissed in the font of holy water. And what else? the inquisitor asked, nodding to his assistant, who tightens, tightens the screws. What else? they plead, their brains so filled with pain they have no room left for lies. Isn't that enough? What more did we do? they plead. The inquisitor nods again to his assistant. What more did you do? Finally he asks, didn't you then have sexual congress with the devil in a female form? Why yes, how could it possibly have slipped our minds? yes, of course, then we all fucked the devil, right there on the holy altar, only—not in a female form.

But now it seems there isn't a single heretic left to torch, and even the Moors are gone, not taken out to sea in ships and sunk, as Philip's grandfather seriously considered, nor slaughtered wholesale, as Philip's father's most trusted advisor counseled him, nor withered away through the castration of all males and the abduction of all children, as more humane voices suggested, but, leaving behind all their worldly goods and chattel and the garb of Christian belief that the Inquisition had forced them to assume, have merely, like the Jews, been expelled. Now they are all gone, those who were supposed to take with them all their treachery and chicanery and leave behind a Spain so pure it would almost rise of its own accord, up, up into the unbearable blue of the Spanish sky, and who instead have left behind this storm's eye of depression, the royal court.

Philip slumps on his throne while the fools and jesters try in vain to bring a smile to his face. Hoping to relieve his imperial boredom, he takes his queen to bed, fantasizing about the pockmarked kitchen girl he has taken a fancy to. Hoping that he has this time impregnated his seventeen-year-old consort with a male but knowing that any child born of such a lustless coupling will be wan and frail, he wanders to Velázquez's studio where he spends the afternoon slumped on a chaise, watching the artist at work and yawning. Sulking Queen

Mariana, who cannot abide Philip's moodiness, who feels that she will go mad if any more of Philip's depression seeps into her, summons Mari Barbola to sit next to him at table.

"Mari," he says, halfway through the supper, "why haven't you said anything to amuse me?"

"I'm hungry," she responds, gnawing at a lamb shank. "So I'm eating."

This remark sends the table into laughter. (Humor is like beer: it doesn't travel. The court fool Borra was said to have killed his master, King Martin, by telling him the following joke: "Out in the vineyard, I saw a young deer hanging by his tail from a tree, as if some one had so punished him for stealing figs." Whereupon the king died of laughter.)

Queen Mariana hoots and slaps her knee, although she has been warned that outright laughter is considered unseemly in the Spanish court, cries out, her speech punctuated at odd intervals by burst of giggles: "Tell me, dear Mari, when you walk in the marketplace, what say the people of our great nation? How fares it?"

"Your Majesty," Mari speaks around mouthfuls of stringy lamb, "in the *mercado* one sees many beggars and many rich people. The beggars implore alms and crusts of bread; yet the rich envy them for at least they have nothing."

"For at least they have nothing . . ." Queen Mariana hoots, and even dour Philip smiles.

"Yes," Mari repeats, blinking and staring coldly at the queen, "because the rich have less than nothing; they owe everywhere, to everyone—"

The queen hoots again and then, gathering her vast skirts in her arms, comes toward Mari, takes her into her arms, lifts her into the air, and kisses her.

The court little people straddle the divide between pets and servants, sometimes acting as living toys, or sometimes frank Cassandras: dogs whose yowling, warning of the coming earthquake, will only be understood when it is too late.

Oh, the bankrupt splendor of the Spanish court! There is no money, not a single *real*; the royal archives are filled with obsequiously worded petitions demanding back wages from maidservants and grooms; yet there is no decrease in the number of maidservants and grooms or in the finery in which they are arrayed: like every servant in Spain, they go about clad in silks and linens which they pay for in coins of air. A dinner is given for Philip and his queen by one of his nobles, and one of the thousand dishes served is a stew which contains one calf, four sheep, two hundred pigeons, a hundred partridges, a hundred rabbits, one thousand pigs' trotters and one thousand tongues, two hundred fowls, thirty hams, and five hundred sausages. Yet a few months later a capon is served to the Infanta Maria Theresa and her half-sister, Margarita, which the infanta orders removed from their presence as it stinks like a dead dog; instead she is served chicken on fingers of toast, which arrives covered with a mantle of buzzing flies. Maria Theresa gags, slaps the hand of the hungry Margarita who stretches out her hand for the chicken, then weeps. There's nothing else in the kitchen, and the shopkeepers refuse to extend any further credit. Mari Barbola lets Maria Theresa carry on for a while, weeping and wailing and gnashing her teeth, before Mari pulls off her ring, a ring that the Infante Baltasar Carlos traded her for a sweet bun when he was four years old. The adults were so amused they allowed her to keep it. She holds the ring aloft between thumb and forefinger, then strides out into the street, returning shortly with the apron of her skirt full of oranges and hams and loaves of bread, a sweet bun. (For once a loan has not only been repaid to the Spanish court but repaid with interest.)

What has happened to Moctezuma's ransom, to the past of the Aztecs and their subject nations, the rings and sacred tablets and gold skulls that were melted down into bars of pure gold? Some say that it passes through the hand of this official and that bureaucrat, dribbling steadily away as it moves, and then goes abroad to pay the interest on the usurious loans that were taken out during the glory days of Spain and to buy silk purses, linen collars that the sumptuary laws forbid the making of in Spain. Some say that no sooner does the plunder of America arrive in Spain then it is returned to the earth from which it was wrenched, reinterred to be safe from the tax collectors. For this the Aztecs and Mayans and Incas are being worked to death in the hot, hot American sun, imploring their dead gods in Nahutal and Maya and Quechua?

But now Mari Barbola has been summoned to the royal gallery for a sitting (some sitting! Velázquez leaves them on their feet all day, even the five-year-old Margarita, and poor Doña Mariana Sarmiento who has to balance herself, kneeling and holding forth a golden tray). Stand here. Stand there. Yes. No, no, more to the left. Your Most Royal Highness might want to take a step to the right. Perfect! José Nieto, master of the royal tapestry works, and the king and queen don't have to hang about posing: they appear in the painting but will be added in later. It's Mari Barbola and Nicolasico Pertusato and the maids of honor who can be ordered to wait about and the infanta, who must, after all, be taught to have the desires of others be her desires, so that at the age of fifteen she can be handed over as wife to the German emperor.

In the painting the embellished cross of the Order of Santiago appears on Velázquez's breast, but it was added afterward, reportedly by the king himself. When he paints *Las meninas* he is petitioning for admission to that order. A report, which takes 113 days to prepare and for which 148 witnesses are sworn and deposed, decrees that Velázquez has successfully proved that his lineage is untainted by Moorish or Jewish blood; yet he is unsuccessful in his claim to have sprung from noble lineage (after all, Daddy, although he called himself a merchant, was really a huckster, rushing about Seville buying dear and selling cheap, and couldn't even call himself Don), no matter that his family insisted that the de Silvas, from whence his father sprung, were descended from Aeneas Silvius, king of Alba Longa and were thus related to the kings of Leon. A dispensation from His Holiness Pope Alexander VII is needed so that Velázquez can be, at last, be sworn into that order that he has so long coveted.

Endless treatises will be written about this painting. One tome sets forth, in the third of its appendices, a sampling of the pigments that were used in it, identification of said pigments having been made via polarizing microscopy, x-ray powder diffraction, and x-ray fluorescence analysis using either a scanning electron microscope or electron beam microprobe. For instance, the light brown stretcher support of the canvas near the lower-left corner is painted with lead white (with a percentage of hydrocerussite somewhere in the range of 40 to 60 percent), yellow ochre, charcoal/bone black,

49

calcite, smalt, and perhaps red ochre or vermilion; while Nicolasico Pertusato's left stocking is lead white, vermilion, red lake, calcite, and charcoal/bone black. Others will plot the geometric relationships between the figures that occupy this space, drawing triangles, equilateral and isosceles, some that reach beyond the frame of the painting.

The king and queen are there but not there, pale reflections in the milk glass of a distant mirror; while Doña Marcela de Ulloa, dressed in mourning garb that resembles a nun's habit, speaks to another old retainer, both fading back into the shadows. José Nieto, firmly planted in his rectangle of light, the head of the royal tapestry factory whose offspring will be the kings of industry, pauses on the steps that lead away from the darkness that is settling over the Spanish court.

Doña Mariana Sarmiento kneels before the Infanta Margarita, offering her on a little golden tray a cup of water in a red *bucaro*, a cup made of soft clay from South America, clay gathered from muddy riverbanks by Indians who have seen their sisters and brothers burned alive by literal fire or those plagues and poxes that the Europeans brought with them: the special red clay cup that, when empty, can be chewed and swallowed. The infanta is about to reach out her hand and drink the blood and sweat, eat the dead flesh of her American subjects.

Nicolasico Pertusato sets his foot on the drowsy Alsatian recumbent at his feet, sets his foot on the uneasy divide between the human and the animal, us and them, while Mari Barbola, frank and ugly Mari Barbola, stares out from the edge of the canvas at us: Look, she says. Look. Here. This is the way it was. Look.

Seventy-five years later an underpaid lackey in the kitchen allows a flame too close to a vat of oil. When he sees what he has done, he sneaks from the Alcazar and sits that night in a tavern, nursing a bottle of thick red wine while he hears the shouts of *Fire! Fire! Fire!* and the out-of-breath gossip delivered by those who have just come from the yards around the court. The fire has climbed worn velvet curtains, lapped up carved mahogany tables and silk brocades; the infantas and the ladies-in-waiting have hitched up their skirts and run pell-mell for the doors, dashing alongside scullery maids and courtiers and the king. Outside the royal family catches its collective breath and then orders the servants back in to fetch jewels and gold and strands of pearls (the pretty globes found lodged in clamshells that the *mga katutubo* used to dive for late in the afternoon, roll about in their palms, and perhaps leave lying in the sand, that the *Kastila* are ready to risk their lives for). The lucky ones return with sweat running down their faces, wheezing, carrying jewelry boxes, fortunes stuffed in their pockets, or staggering under the weight of the immense canvases, the paint blistering and running in the heat of the fire. From across the way, where the painting has been borne for safety, paint runs down Mari Barbola's doughy face as she stares out at the frantic racing, the flames surging higher and higher through the doomed palace of the Alcazar.

Two hundred and twelve years after the burning of the Alcazar, 287 years after Velázquez painted *Las meninas*, outside a town in Poland 1,232 kilometers from Madrid, a man in a military uniform speaks to a woman wearing thin pajamas.

"You see—the problem with the photographs," he says

shaking them out of the manila file and onto his desk. They stand, not exactly side by side, but as a junior clerk might stand in the presence of the owner of a firm.

"Now you see, this one—she had a very interesting texture to her skin, a certain kind of fat deposit underneath her chin," he tugs at the flesh of his own neck to indicate, "which the camera doesn't capture at all." In an irritated whisper he adds, "That shivering is most annoying. Stop it."

She stops. So much for what her professors had said about involuntary movement. Or perhaps it was just that at that place, in that time, the laws of nature had also been suspended.

"And then this one," he says, throwing down a photograph of a fat dwarf with an outsized head, "he had sexual organs like a child's, but again the camera—"

"The camera's eye is flat. It captures everything and so, sometimes, fails to see the essential." She knows she is taking an enormous risk in saying these words, which might be read as insolent. On the other hand, sometimes cowering, putting one's tail between one's legs, didn't work either. Every day in this place you engaged in a game of Russian roulette, holding a gun to your head, never certain if the words you spoke would allow you to live for a while longer or trigger your death. That, of course, was just a figure of speech: the real gun was always in their hands.

"Precisely," he says.

She is about to say, "When I was a medical illustrator in Prague . . ." and mention the name of a famous doctor she had worked with, but she decides against it, merely looks at the floor and mumbles, "I was a medical illustrator in Prague."

"Oh, that's good. Very good. I didn't know that. Come along. You can get started right away. The doctors will let you know if there's some feature they want emphasized."

She is following him down the hallway when he adds, "Also, there's the matter of the cost of the photographic process." And laughs a little at his own joke. Only his way of letting her know that although they are walking down the corridor together, although she made an observation to which he responded, "Precisely," she is worth less than the thin layer of emulsion that is spread over film, worth less than a few *pfennigs*' worth of developing salts.

A man in a white coat joins them. She is led to a cubicle.

Usually the dwarfs are brought in by an orderly; occasionally it is a doctor who accompanies them, when he has some special instruction he wants to give the illustrator, whose given name is Dina, although it has been months now since anyone has called her by her given name. The dwarfs arrive quite naked and yet they never seem ashamed.

Once someone left a chair here, and for a few days Dina was able to sit down as she worked. Her body has long since gnawed up the fat of its own belly, its own breasts, and turned finally to the fat that padded the balls of her heel, leaving a raw pain between heel bone and ground.

And then one day the chair is gone.

Sometimes the door of the cubicle is left open; sometimes it is closed. Although Dina prefers that it be closed, she never shuts it herself.

Sometimes the doctors bring her an inch or two of soup in a coffee mug, a napkin holding a scrap of bread. It is against the rules. But they like her work; they don't want to lose her to typhoid or cholera.

Usually it is quite straightforward: front, rear, left side, right side. She doesn't speak to them, except to ask them to turn. What can they possibly say to each other? Sometimes she is told to do a more detailed sketch: of a patient's genitalia or of a deformity.

The doctor holds Lia Graf's hand as they came down the corridor. She smiles up at him as he bends down and lifts her up onto the table. Dina has never seen a doctor touch one of them before.

"Today we have a celebrity for you. From—" and he begins to laugh.

"The Barnum & Bailey Circus, the Greatest Show on Earth."

"Barnum & Bailey," he repeats, his German accent turning the words into guttural commands. "And she became quite a little celebrity when she sat on the lap of J. P. Morgan. The usual four sketches."

"Good-bye, Doctor," she trills, but he makes no response. She is perfectly proportioned, roughly two-thirds of a meter tall. Instinctively, no doubt because of her theatrical background, she assumes a somewhat coquettish stance. She is in her mid-thirties. Warts on her elbows. One missing tooth. But otherwise quite well preserved.

"No. Don't pose. Just stand there. Arms at your sides. And please turn around." Dina dislikes doing the front views; she always does them last.

Lia turns her head over her shoulder and mouths: "What is your name?"

After a nearly thirty seconds' pause, the answer is mouthed back. "Dina."

"Lia Graf . . . Where are you from?"

"Prague," she whispers.

"Wiesbaden." Then: "How long?"

"Just stand there," Dina says aloud. "Your head as it was. I cannot draw you properly if you don't hold still."

"Please. It's important for me. To know."

"Quiet," Dina says, and draws her finger across her throat.

Dina works in silence until the evening siren sounds. Then she is returned to the barracks and Lia Graf to the ward.

The next morning they resume. The doctor doesn't bring her this morning, but instead a nurse, dressed in white. Dina is the one who hoists her onto the table. The nurse closes the door behind him.

"Your left side now."

After a few minutes Lia says, certainly not in a normal speaking voice but not in the barely audible whisper of the day before: "The door is closed. Will you not talk to me now?"

"I talk to no one. It distracts me."

"Distracts you from your drawing?"

"No. From staying alive."

"But I talk to you because I want to live."

"Everyone wants to live. They all wanted to live." The cubicle is windowless, so she cannot gesture to the plume of smoke. Instead she wrinkles her nose at the stench in the air. And then makes a sound. What shall we call it: laughter, a hoot, a snort? Any of those will do equally well, or poorly. Ordinary language is another thing that does not fare well here.

"You are cruel."

"I am alive."

"So am I. And I am going to go on living."

Dina laughs again. "How long have you been here?"

"Don't mistake me for a child. We are used to that assumption. We often turn it to our advantage. I was arrested in '38."

"'38. It is I who should be trying to get you to talk. Tell me your secret."

"Be a dwarf. They call it a sign of degeneracy, inferiority, but in this world they have made it is a distinct advantage. I do not thrive on the rations they give us, but I can survive."

"'38," the artist repeats.

"A 'useless person.' I had been working in a revue. You know, torch singers and jazz and an—the English expression is 'off-color'—an off-color comedian. And me. I was billed as 'Lia Graf: The Miniature Sensation.' I wore a top hat and tails and sang ribald songs. They loved me, the audiences. A woman who after all isn't really a woman, after all, she's a dwarf dressed like a man and gives us the pleasure of allowing us to lust without guilt after a child, a man, a woman. Sang? Really, I couldn't carry a tune. A pianist played and I half sang, half spoke in a gravelly pseudo-Dietrich. But we sapped the strength of the German people. We were decadent. Foreign. Cosmopolitan. But it wouldn't have mattered for me—whatever kind of show I was in. At that time we were forbidden altogether from appearing on the stage. So then I was a 'useless mouth' and imprisoned. But I always managed to find myself a protector. To become someone's mascot. And they wanted to study us." She allows a few moments to pass and utters, "Ah, why did I ever leave America?"

Dina does not rise to the bait.

"That circus. You can't imagine what it was like: the stink from all those animals. And I never got a decent night's sleep there: the elephants bellowing and the lions roaring, not to mention the goddamn hyena. Night after night, all night long. So when I got the offer from the revue . . . The money was better. I was homesick. Tired of speaking English. Barnum was so goddamn tightfisted. I thought, Things are bad in Germany; they're bad in America. So I came back in '35."

"'35?"

"Politics bored me."

"Fool."

She whirls around: "Let me tell you something. When they've had you for as long as they've had me, you can tell who's going to survive and who isn't. When I look at you, Dina, I see a skull."

"As you were."

"And what if I don't?"

"Back as you were."

She sits down on the table. "What do they do with these drawings?"

"They go in your file. Along with the medical records, the genealogy, and the autopsy report."

"Dr. Baumgarten is very fond of me."

"Yes, you are his little pet. But time is taking its toll on you. Your flesh is sagging and soon your hair will turn gray. Then you will be old: perhaps not old in outside years but old in Auschwitz years, which pass much more quickly than the years of a dog's life. Remember that even the most loving families, although they may be shedding tears as they do it, put pets to sleep."

"One-two-three-four. You know how they love order. If step three is not completed, step four cannot be."

"Stand up. As you were."

"No."

"If I tell them that you are refusing to pose—"

"I will tell them that you tried to enlist me in a seditious plot."

"All you will succeed in doing is sending me up in smoke. They will find someone else to do the drawings."

Lia looks at Dina, prepared to match her glare, an eye for an angry eye. But Dina only looks hollowly at her, the dull unfocused stare of people back in the other world when they wait in bus terminals, wait.

Lia rises to her feet, resumes her pose. "Talk to me."

Her voice is as hollow as her stare. "I'm Czech. A Jew."

"Yes?"

"That's all."

"No. There's more."

"I draw the pictures here in the hospital."

"Yes?"

"That's all."

"I'll call the guard. Tell him about the plot you tried to enlist me in."

"They won't believe you."

"It won't matter whether they believe me or not. They'll kill you just to be on the safe side."

"I was born in Prague . . ." she begins. An old, familiar story: The grandparents still living in the ghetto, in the dark rooms of the past with their heavy curtains and their flickering Sabbath candles. Her grandparents had believed the old tale about the two white doves that for over a millennia had come and perched on the roof of the synagogue to save it from fire; yes, and believed too that there was an underground tunnel leading straight from the Old Jewish Town to Jerusalem. Right up until March 15, 1938, they had believed these things. Her parents did not believe any such fairy tales; no, they believed that their Jewishness was a coat they could slip out of and hang on a convenient hook, to put on again when they chose. Her mother even took Dina to the Mala Strana at Christmas to see the pastry angels with their wings of spun sugar set out in the windows of the bakery shop: the quaint customs of the Christians. For a second, as Dina speaks, she smells not the smell that was everywhere in that place, but the smell of cinnamon, the smell of fresh snow, the smell of the tram wheels as they spark to a stop.

"Yes," Lia says, "go on."

"That's all."

"Go on." Lia says. "That's all."

"Go on."

"What do you hope to accomplish by this?"

"It helps me understand."

"This? You will never understand this."

"I think I almost do. Go on," Lia orders.

Lia, you can see what this is doing to her. Why are you insisting so? It's not as if there were something unusual about this story. It could be the story of any of a hundred, a thousand, a million other sensitive girls with souls that aspired beyond the quotidian. The desire to be an artist, the mother who nurtured her dreams and the father who mocked her. She compromised, agreed to study medical illustration as well. And four years after she graduated, during the terrible winter of '31, working days doing drawings for medical professors, nights her own work, she saw the boy wunderkind who had sat next to her in life drawing class hauling coal and turned away before he could see her and so be ashamed. Nights and weekends she painted her pictures of robust young girls from the country she hired as models. You've seen this play before, Lia, you know the final act: the god of death goose-steps out of a trapdoor in the floor of the stage and puts an end to all this silly palavering about the soul of the artist.

But you say, "Go on."

She's furious now, Lia. That hand that once patiently delineated the coils and flutings of a bacterium now presses the pencil so hard it engraves the paper.

"Go on," she says. "Tell me about the beautiful country girls you drew. Go on. I think I almost understand this."

The paintings Dina made in Prague are gone, chucked out by the German-speaking Czechs who took over her family's house. A few prewar photos of Lia Graf remain: publicity stills, the photographs the newsmen shot after they set her on J. P. Morgan's lap, but most of the pictures of her are gone, gone up in smoke like Lia and Dina themselves. In a brown manila envelope kept shut by a twisted piece of string on a dusty shelf in an archive are the four drawings Dina made of Lia, left side, right side, rear, front (is she really almost smiling?) along with the medical report, the genealogy, and the autopsy report.

Comrade Luxemburg and Comrade Gramsci Pass Each Other at a Congress of the Second International in Switzerland on the 10th of March, 1912

Italicized sections of the text are quotations from Johann Goethe, Rosa Luxemburg, Johnny Cash, Alfred Döblin, Antonio Gramsci, Vladimir Lenin, Benito Mussolini, Adolf Hitler, Karl Koch, and the Bible.

It never happened.

It could not have happened.

It could not have happened that at a crowded congress of the Second International held in a resort hotel on the shores of Lake Catani in the foothills of the Swiss Alps, alongside a snow-fed lake with waters of such pure crystalline blue that even in the very center one could peer straight down and clearly see the fluid shadows of the waters' ripples speckling the rocks at the bottom, the delegates from the socialist parties of the world gathering in clots in the hallways, doing the real business of the congress there with urgent imprecations, hands grasping forearms, voices dropped almost to whispers and glances over their shoulders, while upstairs

61

an overworked chambermaid with varicose veins, Madame Robert, flicked a sheet in the air, sending motes of dust dancing in the afternoon sunshine, Comrade Rosa Luxemburg and Comrade Antonio Gramsci limped past each other.

It never happened that Luxemburg, who had been detained after her speech by those anxious to get her advice, to give her theirs, to merely say that they had spoken with her, yes, individually, personally, at last signaled to her companion with her eyes, who worked his way through the knot of people surrounding her, laid a paternal hand on her arm, said, "Rosa, you must . . ." and Rosa allowed herself to be led away, departing the Geneva Room at 2:52 in the afternoon, while at 2:51 Comrade Gramsci had sneezed, futilely searched his pockets for a handkerchief, and, having wiped his nose surreptitiously with the back of his hand, bowed his head and hurried through the crowded corridor to ascend to his room on the fifth floor to fetch one, so that, two-thirds of the way along, the two of you would pass each other.

No, it could not have happened.

On March 10, 1912, at eight minutes before 3:00 in the afternoon, Rosa Luxemburg was in her apartment on Lindenstrasse in Berlin, preparing a lecture for the Party School, thumbing through Goethe's *Faust*, looking for the quotation *No one yields empire / To another; no one will yield it who has gained it by force* . . . the same volume that she will drop into her purse when she hears the footsteps coming up the stairs of the house in Neukölln to take her to her death six years later; and Gramsci was a twenty-one-year-old, a poverty-stricken Sardinian student, eating his first meal in three days, a plate of *spaghetti con olio*, at a trattoria on the Via Perugia in Turin, reading a linguistics text as he ate at a table just a little bit too high for him, so that his arms ached slightly from the odd angle at which they had to be maneuvered. At the next table a father moaned and patted his belly, pushed his chair back from the table, then urged his plump daughters to eat desert, accompanying his coaxings with tugs at their flesh: they were too thin, altogether too thin, his dumplings, his darlings. The coy daughters protested; the *padre* signaled the waiter to clear away the platters of calamari and pasta, the remains of the spring lamb, the half flask of wine. Later, limping home alone in a sharp wind with his half-empty belly (why does one feel the cold so much more when one is hungry?), Gramsci tried to name the force that allowed him to watch the remains of the rich man's dinner being taken away while he still hungered: a dog, a dumb brute, would have leapt for it, seized the lamb in his teeth. The dog would have been a better socialist than I am, he thought.

No, Comrade Luxemburg does not pass Comrade Gramsci as she heads down the corridor on her way to sit next to Karl Liebknecht at dinner, on her way to dine with him and twelve Judases, on her way to *the unprecedented, the incredible 4th of August, 1914,* when the men she thought of as her comrades will vote for war appropriations so that the workers of Germany can kill and in turn be killed by the workers of Italy and France and England; on her way to the gloomy evening a few weeks later when she and Clara Zetkin will sit in her parlor, four feet in scuffed slippers resting on the fender before the fire, debating not the woman question, not organizational questions of the party but whether laudanum or prussic acid would be a better way to go because *mass murder has become a boring monotonous daily business*; on her way to listening to the whistle of the 3:19 train carrying

Mathilde away from her in the prison where she was locked up for her opposition to the war (*If they freed me from this prison / if that railroad train was mine / you bet I'd move it on / a little further down the line / far from Folsom Prison*); she will promise Sonja Liebknecht to go to Corsica with her after the war (*On high, nothing except barren rock formations which are a noble gray; below, luxuriant olive trees, cherry trees, and age-old chestnut trees. And above everything, a prehistoric quiet—no human voices, no bird calls, only a stream rippling somewhere between rocks, or the wind on high whispering between the cliffs—still the same wind that swelled Ulysses' sails*), but she will never see Corsica again; instead she will spend her first night of freedom, a sleepless night, at the railway workers' union hall, preparing for a demonstration the next day; on her way to Berlin, where red flags will be flying everywhere (*precisely when on the surface everything seems hopeless and miserable, a complete change is getting ready*); on her way to her dazed, lurching walk through the corridors of the Hotel Eden (*You know I really hope to die at my post, in a street fight or in prison*), past the chambermaids and valets who, a few weeks previously, might have joined the throngs in the streets of Berlin, might even have had a sister or brother who took part in the occupation of the Vorwärts building, demanding of a newcomer, "*Why have you come so late? And why have you not brought others with you?*", who will now join in the jeering: Jew, sow, red whore, cripple, Jew; on her way to the black car, on her way to the bullet to her brain that pierces her left temporal lobe and wipes out the throne within her brain where reason sat; on her way to becoming, for a few brief minutes, no longer Dr. Luxemburg, no longer the visionary, the prophet, just a body, an unconscious (*sometimes it seems to me that I am not really a human being at all, but rather a bird or a beast in human form*); a body whose dead weight will plummet into the waters of the Landwehr Canal.

She does not pass Comrade Gramsci on his way to his room on the fifth floor to fetch a handkerchief; on his way to the Petrograd train station, where he will be met by a delegation of four men and one woman who will stand on the platform scanning the air above him, and he will pretend not to notice the few seconds' lag after he announces himself in a voice he has made as deep as possible (this shrunken hunchback the famous leader?—sometimes they will have been warned ahead of time that he is *handicapped, deformed,* but then they will expect some Cyclops, a Minotaur, not this limping dwarf); on his way to being led into the courtroom, where everyone save the prisoners will appear in tragicomic fascist splendor, a double cordon of militiamen in plumed black helmets, heels of well-polished shoes clicked together, backs straight, an emblematic dagger poised in an identical position in the belt of each one, the marshals bearing standards that read SPQR, Senatus Populusque Romanarum—of course, this will recall to him Marx's comment about history repeating itself, the first time as tragedy and the second as farce; he will limp in dirty, unshaven, feeling like a wounded, crawling animal: a ferret, perhaps, slithering and predatory; he will feel a sense of physical shame and understand again a sentence he will have written years before when the Turin workers councils failed: *the bourgeoisie lies in ambush in the hearts of the proletariat;* on his way to becoming the great mind, the Gramsci who floats, a head without a body, on fading posters once thumbtacked to apartment walls in

Madison, Wisconsin, and Berkeley, California, now matted and framed.

Rosa, you warned us, *we can no more skip a period in our historical development than a man can jump over his shadow.* But still I spray-paint on the walls of the Hotel Leveque a slogan that wouldn't be heard for fifty-odd years hence: "All power to the imagination!" I imagine that in those days when we didn't yet have a name for ourselves, when the only words were *handicapped, lame, deformed, hunchback, dwarf, cripple*, when the only words were silence, that we could speak.

I imagine that Comrade Luxemburg stares, looks away, but then laughs at herself for doing so: not out loud, not a full-throated, rich deep laugh, but only a laugh of mild amusement at her "instinctive" reaction. And then she turns, smiles, as you or I might do, passing each other in the corridor at a meeting filled with ABS.

She stops, stretches out her hand, says, "We haven't met. I'm Rosa Luxemburg."

"Of course," he mutters, "yes, of course," stretching out his hand in return, conscious of the fact that it's the one he used in the absence of a handkerchief.

"And you?" she says, helping out the flustered young man. He gives his name. "Let's talk," she says.

After dinner when the coffee's served, they meet out on the veranda. Of course the stone benches out there are backless, and so they'll schlep three chairs out—one to prop their feet on, which otherwise would dangle above the ground.

"So," Rosa asks right out, "has your disability made difficulties for you, in the party?"

Antonio shrugs. "They—the workers—trust me."

She nods, she knows. The wound on the outside, so that strangers on a train pick you to tell their tale to.

"But they fear it, too," she supplies.

"Yes, they fear it, too."

"And yet," she says, "I often wonder if I would have got as far in the party as I have if it weren't for—"

"The de-sexualization—"

"De-gendering was more what I was going to say," she says. Because of all those years of her growing up when it seemed that she was destined to be permanently outside the realm of desire, his words make her a bit prickly. If she were honest with herself about this—although she couldn't be—she'd admit that it was one of the things that led her to socialism: that it was the place where her strength of mind, of character could overcome her physical flaw, allow her to be desired. She only lets herself know that she felt freedom here, a freedom she couldn't feel anywhere else.

Comrades, I want you to go on but this conversation has grown awkward, studded with anachronisms, impossible to write. All power to the imagination? As difficult a slogan to put into practice as *All power to the soviets.*

And although I want to holler back through time: "Please, speak to each other," I cannot let you know what's to come. Mussolini is not yet a fascist, he has not yet become a man of steel, a man who will slap cold water on raw morning flesh, his chest puffed out like an enormous steam engine; *the masses are a woman,* he will say, and, at a certain moment when haranguing them from a balcony he feels their submissive spirit reach up toward him, he will strip off his shirt to show those muscles like iron bands, jut forward that great leonine head, the lumpishness of his bald skull giving the effect of a

Roman head chiseled in marble. Hitler is still nothing more than a gleam in the evil eye of history. He has not yet spun that web of propaganda wherein disease, prostitution, the kaftaned Jew lurking in the alley waiting to defile the Aryan woman, *the suffocating perfume of our modern eroticism*, the degenerates contaminating the healthy and passing on their defective genes to their offspring blur together and become one. He has not yet declared that Germany must become a healthy state. Kommandant Koch of Buchenwald has not yet said, *There are no sick men in my camp. They are all either well or dead.* Mussolini, Hitler, Koch will understand: the worship of the healthy body, the fear of us, is the taproot of fascism.

But Rosa, sober Rosa, leans forward through time to reprimand me: *In the beginning was the act.* No, they can't yet speak to each other. We don't yet exist. We are the sons and daughters of fascism as well as the daughters and sons of ourselves.

So I try again. I fast-forward through the next four bloody years of history: the soldiers look like Keystone Kops as they rush out of their trenches, grimace, fall to the ground, and the next wave of soldiers rises and does the same, and the next does the same, and the next does the same and the next does the same and the next does the same, until some 22 million have died and I hit the "play" button and return to normal speed.

Rosa walks out the doors of Breslau Prison, she speaks at the rally in Berlin, she writes, *There is order in Berlin . . . your order is built on sand.* But she never takes that last dazed, lurching walk through the corridors of the Hotel Eden; she never is found, a bloated marshmallow of a corpse, eyeless, bobbing against the locks of the Landwehr Canal. Instead she escapes to the Soviet Union, from there she hopscotches to New York. Antonio, at first I imagine that you were persuaded to leave Italy before your arrest, but even in the world of the imagination I can't wish *The Prison Notebooks*, the *Letters*, out of existence. Forgive me, Nino, but I am sending you into that first filthy cell in Regina Coeli Prison, where the single bare bulb burns all night long and the lice scuttle through the mattress—and into all the prison cells that followed that one. Let's suppose that Romain Rolland, who has worked so diligently for your release all these years—circulating petitions, writing endless letters, lobbying in the court of world opinion—despairs of those tactics: instead, knowing how close you are to death, he organizes a commando raid against the Quisisana Clinic. Chuck Norris is the advance man, he disguises himself as a taciturn (male) nurse—we'll explain away his fair complexion by having him pretend to be German; at the appointed hour, while a helicopter lowers itself toward the roof, he'll pick you up in his arms like a baby (you weighed only forty-two kilograms then), toss you over his shoulder and, a machine gun in his free hand, taking out a few fascists as he rushes to the roof. Chuck will cradle you in his arms, stroke your black hair away from your hot forehead, say, "Hey, guy, it's okay. You're all right, Comrade." There will be no flyer headlined "Italian Fascism Has Murdered Gramsci." No, Comrade, you will live.

Neither of them will become famous. Sorry, there's truth to that old saw about death being good for your career. Rosa ends up giving lectures at the New School, writing for magazines with ever-dwindling circulations. She began her article

"Either/Or" with a quote from Revelations: *I would thou wert cold or hot. So then because thou art lukewarm, and neither cold nor hot, I will spew thee out of my mouth.* But now the masses have moved to White Plains, they drive DeSotos, she has become an apocalyptic crank. Antonio sits out the war years in the warm dry air of southern California, regaining some measure of health, joining up with that colony of squabbling, quibbling, squalling leftist exiles.

What will I do with them now that I've saved them? Have them meet again, on a subway platform in Brooklyn, Rosa, 103, with that papery, almost smooth-as-a-baby's patch of skin on her cheeks that old, old women get; and Antonio, in his eighties, lumbering and wheezing up the steps. But then, it could only be the early 1970s: too early still. No, I'll have time pass but the two of them stay in their late forties, the ages they were when they died; it's 1990: Rosa is sitting on the bench at Ditmas station in Brooklyn, waiting for the F train, the Americans with Disabilities Act has just passed; she's reading the article about it in the *New York Times*. Antonio comes and sits down next to her. He knows enough to leave a couple of New York inches between the two of them, but still she sidles a bit away. He can't help looking over her shoulder, reading the same article she is. She shakes the newspaper a bit, casts him a quick cold glance. He looks away; but then she says, "Excuse me. We've met, haven't we?"

What shall I have the two of them say? Shall I have Antonio say that our movement must concern itself with more than legislation, *must reach for the solution to more complex tasks than those proposed by the present development of the struggle; namely, for the creation of a new, integral culture*; shall

I have Rosa come back with the necessity of our movement being democratic, that we must make our own *errors, errors . . . infinitely more fruitful and more valuable than the infallibility* of any CIL board and all its high-powered consultants?

But no, it's another conversation I can't imagine.

No, I have to go back to that hotel corridor.

Although it could not have happened that on the 10th of March, 1912, at a congress of the Second International in a corridor of the Hotel Leveque at precisely 2:52, that Comrade Luxemburg, heading in a southerly direction down the corridor toward the dining hall, while Comrade Gramsci, headed toward the north staircase, passed each other, still, had it happened, Rosa would have startled slightly as she glimpsed him, the misshapen dwarf limping toward her in a secondhand black suit so worn the fabric was turning green with age, her eye immediately drawn to this disruption in the visual field. Realizing she was staring, she would have glanced quickly away. And then the moment after, realizing that the quick aversion of her gaze was as much of an insult as the stare, she would have turned her head back but tried to make her gaze general. Comrade Rosa would have felt a slight flicker of embarrassment? shame? revulsion? dread? of a feeling that can have no name?

Would Gramsci at first have bowed his head in shame, then raised his head, stared back, deciding that her right to look at him equaled his right to look at her? Did a slight smile pass across his face because he was glad to know that such a prominent comrade shared his condition?

It is all over in a matter of seconds.

But this never happened, and even if it had, it would have not have mattered. What passed between the two of you belongs to the realm of thought before speech, of the shape of the future before it can be seen: a nameless discomfort, not yet even a premonition.

No, there is no such place on earth. You will not find this Lake Catani on any map: I have created it out of words. This congress never happened; the two of you were not there.

Look down through those clear blue waters of Lake Catani to the shifting shadows of the lake's ripples that speckle the rocks at the bottom; see the shadows grow larger and larger until they dissolve into nothingness; now the lake itself, which never existed, disappears. The scullery girl chopping onions in the kitchen automatically wipes her cheeks with the backs of her hands and discovers that her cheeks are not wet with onion tears; surprised, she sniffs the air: it does not smell of onions, it does not smell of anything. Upstairs, the chambermaid, old Madame Robert, stands on her aching legs and snaps a freshly laundered sheet through the air. Madame Robert, your legs will ache no more: I am writing away your pain, I am writing away your very existence. For a moment the motes of dust you have disturbed dance glistening in the air, but then they cease, and first the sheet itself and then you yourself turn to shadows and vanish.

Gloucester

I am propped up in my hospital bed, reading the *New York Times*, as I have every day of my life since the age of ten. Although my eyes are burning, I read. A war criminal has evaded capture in Bosnia. One former Kennedy wife complains of the manner in which she was disposed; another stands loyally alongside her philandering husband. The Dow Jones may soon break eight thousand. The Red Sox have beaten the Tigers. I can manage only the headlines, but still I read.

A doctor enters.

"So, Mr. Gloucester," he says, setting his hand not on my shoulder but on the bed next to my shoulder. Then he reaches behind him for the chair.

"First name's Gloucester," I tell him. "Remember?"

We had this conversation yesterday, word for word, gesture for gesture. I remember, although I'm the one with dementia. He's allowed to forget: he's a busy man. I was once a busy man, and I forgot things: names of housekeepers, names of men with whom I'd had brief encounters, shall we say, once my son Charlie's birthday.

"Oh, right," he says, "right, right. Sure. Yeah."

I suppose when he got into this field he was like Sisyphus pushing the rock up the mountain. Then one day, incredibly, the rock stayed up at the summit. Just a few loose pebbles came cascading down. I'm one of the loose pebbles. At the AIDS Resource Center they are having a workshop on reentering the workforce: Thursday evenings from 7:00 to 10:00 a group called Lazarus meets. I will not be reentering the workforce; I will not be joining the Thursday evening group.

"Mr. Uh—"

"Barrows."

"Any relation to the senator?" he asks, chuckling.

"He's my brother," I say, and his fingers, which are right then in the middle of palpating the lymph nodes in my neck, pause for a deferential second.

The doctor is a numbers man. He does not put his hand on my shoulder and attempt to make eye contact. I am grateful for this. 47, he says to me, telling me the results of some test from the printout in his hand. 22. My white blood cell count is holding steady. The Dow Jones is up. My CD4 cells are down.

"Your cholesterol's 150. That's great," he says, and we both laugh.

"I could go eat some lard," I say.

"Häagen-Dazs," he says.

"Well, I guess I don't have to worry about my heart."

"Yeah, well . . . ," he says. He doesn't want to give me any false hope. Anything can happen.

The doctor is telling me another number. The number is
12.

"What's the normal range on that?"

"Somewhere between 10,000 and 15,000."

"And mine's 12?"

"Yeah," the doctor says. "Not 12,000. 12."

"Yes," I say.

"Now about your eyes . . . ," he says.

My ancestors pepper the passenger list of the Mayflower; a
great-great-grandfather gave Henry Adams a black eye, an
event unrecorded in his *Education*. I am not from the most
distinguished branch of the family, I must admit. I am a
younger son, descended of younger sons. My father found
the notion of knotting a piece of silk around his neck and
going out to earn a living a puzzling one. Instead he went to
the Gardner, read the *Times*, and watched his investments.

Between my junior and my senior year at Choate, while
the kids who were from nouveau riche families headed off to
Europe, those of us from solid old families went and worked
at canneries on the Cape or waited tables at restaurants in
Newport. Perhaps Chairman Mao got the idea of sending
intellectuals to live among the peasantry from this Yankee
custom. I worked at a bar in Provincetown. That summer
on the Cape, I learned that other people had middle names
like Ann or Thomas, not fine old family names, names that
couldn't go to waste, as middle or even first names. I gathered
in the kitchen with my coworkers to make fun of the fags. (I
modestly admit I did the best imitations.) A few years later
in a history class at Harvard taught by a junior professor (he
was not given tenure), I learned that via such mockery was

justified class antagonism thwarted. At about the same time in an expensive psychiatrist's office, I was learning exactly why my imitations had been so apt.

During a junior year at Oxford I got the hang of the British way of doing things. Private proclivities could be just that: one could couple dutifully, beget sons (and daughters); heterosexual activity could be like a twice-a-year trip to the dentist.

And what of Patricia, my poor wife? She was not naive. She lacked beauty, charm. I was her chance for making a decent match. She got my name, sons out of her loins. Although I wasn't what one in a court of law would call faithful, still, I kept my compact. Our marriage was loveless, granted, but unlike many of the romantic matches around us, after a few years we had not gone fetid and bitter.

She divorced me shortly after my diagnosis: public humiliation was not part of the bargain.

Sons? Two. (Like most children, my sons probably counted the issue of their generation and thought, They did it twice. They were wrong, of course, but not by much.)

Ah, my sons, my sons!

Pardon me, I grow bathetic. It is an unpleasant side effect of my condition.

But my poor, loony, Charlie! He was sixteen when I had my first opportunistic infection. Charlie found it embarrassing to: (a) have a father; (b) have a father who was dying; (c) have a father who was dying of AIDS.

Dexter, my elder and, I must admit, my more favored child, seems to be weathering this well. There is a gap of nearly a decade between him and Charlie. (The spirit was willing, but the flesh, etc.) Dexter is on the partnership track at Burton, Myers & Dudley.

Charlie is twenty now. He has a band. His band is called Anti-Man.

"Are you lesbians?" I asked.

No, it's an ecology thing. They are in favor of one species becoming extinct: *homo sapiens*. Charlie is a font of information: how many pounds of laundry detergent are used per capita in the United States each year. (Pardon me, I have forgotten the exact figure. The dementia, you know.) Charlie does not wear deodorant; he launders his clothes but rarely; he bathes every other week. Not only is he sparing the environment by this; it is also a consciousness-raising device: our species devotes such enormous effort to escaping its animal origins, and this act—or rather, I should say, omission—reminds us we are merely gussied-up primates.

A neurologist enters my room and asks me to repeat a string of numbers. He asks me to track his moving finger with my eyes. He says, "Okay" and leaves.

At the moment Charlie is in England. He checks in with me weekly via telephone (I pick up the tab). On his most recent call he told me that he had been at Stonehenge, where he dropped acid and watched the sun rise in honor of the summer solstice. He informed me that this was "cosmic" and "heavy, but, you know, not in a bad way." Charlie and I seem to have what psychologists call good communication. My own father was a remote figure. At Charlie's age, had I had any experiences that were either "cosmic" or "heavy"— or both simultaneously—I would have been quite unable to share these with my father.

They are in and out of my room all day: an infectious disease resident, an ophthalmologist, a physical therapist, an occupational therapist, a social worker—she by the name of Ms. Brenda A. O'Malley, the only one among the lot who dresses in clothes like those people in the outside world wear. The rest of them wear pale green scrubs, making them look like children on a Sunday morning playing hospital in their rumpled pajamas while their parents sleep in.

Ms. O'Malley sets her black satchel on the floor and I see that it contains a book called *Appreciating Opera*. Dear Ms. O'Malley wants to improve herself. Forgive me my many petty cruelties, but understand: I must now seize all the opportunities. I will not get to be a garrulous old man. (I wonder if the A. on Ms. O'Malley's name tag stands for Ann.)

Ms. O'Malley is accompanied by someone called the Discharge Planner.

"I don't know," Ms. Brenda A. O'Malley says, "much about your financial circumstances—"

"I've always been comfortable," I say. I allow the word *comfortable* to roll around in my mouth. Does comfortable mean capable of being comforted?

Ms. O'Malley and the Discharge Planner speak with me about spending down. They say that even quite considerable assets can be eaten up.

Munch, munch, munch, I'm a goat out to lunch. It's a line from a book I read the boys when they were little. It cascades through my head all afternoon. Munch, munch, munch, I'm a goat out to lunch.

Later my son Dexter pops in. "I can't stay long," he says, his eyes darting about.

Dexter leans his right ankle against his left knee. "Dad," he says, "I want to ask your input on something! Christ!

What a word! Advice, Dad, I want your advice." Dexter is drumming his fingers against the aquamarine vinyl arm of the chair while he goes on: Rob—there is a lag time of a few seconds while I figure out that this is my brother, the good senator—has suggested that he make a run for the office of attorney general. If my son is elected attorney general, the correct form of address for him will be the Honorable Dexter Barrows. My Dexter!

"Well, Dad, the other thing is—well, money."

Ah, yes.

My lawyer is another numbers man. This many hundreds of thousands here; this many hundreds of thousands there. Sheltered, he says. When he says "trust" he is talking about something which can be established with a wave of a pen. Guardians. Majority. Structure. Assets. Closely held corporations. Durable power of attorney. He also talks about something referred to as "in the event of your—uh—"

I call my progeny together: faithful son and prodigal, who has cut short his English adventure to return to my bedside. Dexter arrives first, interrupting a book I am listening to on tape. I can no longer read. Read print, as Ms. O'Malley would say.

I had several mistaken impressions about this process of going blind. I thought it was going to be Keatsian. I thought the light would fade, grow dimmer and dimmer and then flicker wanly out. But no, it's quite Byronic. Dexter comes in and sees me sitting in the dark, switches on the light.

"Christ, no. Jesus-God." I put my hands over my eyes. "The light!"

"What?" he says. "What?"

"Turn off the fucking light!" I shout.

"Christ, Dad," he says. The swearing in each other's presence is new. Then: "Sorry," more annoyed than repentant. "What's up with your eyes?"

"I'm feeling a little better today. Overall. I think. How're things going with you?"

"Fine," Dexter says. "Dad. How about your eyes?"

"The infection isn't responding to treatment," I say.

"What does that mean?" Dexter asks.

"It means I am going blind."

"Oh, God," Dexter says. He folds himself double, pounds his fists on the edges of the orange plastic chair in which he is seated. "Oh, Jesus. Oh, fuck," he says.

"Dexter," I say. "Dexter. I'm sorry—"

"Dad," he interrupts me. "This guy that's treating you: are you sure he's good?"

"Yes," I say. "He's very highly thought of."

"Yeah, okay," Dexter says. "But will you just get a second opinion?"

Poor Dexter. He just cannot believe that all my wit, all my urbanity, all my cultivation, all my money, all my taste, all my connections, all my breeding—none of those things will help me now.

The other issue of my loins enters my room: shaggy, redolent, muttish, ruttish.

"Don't turn on the light," Dexter warns. "Dad's eyes . . ."

"Hey, bro," Charlie says, hitting Dexter's arm.

"Hey, man," Dexter says. "How was Europe?"

Charlie leans over and kisses me. He bicycled to the hospital from his shared house in Somerville, and a droplet of sweat drips off his face and onto mine.

"What's up with your eyes?"

"By my lusts were my eyes put out . . ."

"He has an infection. It's not responding to treatment. He's going to get a second opinion."

"Dad," Charlie chides, "it's cool that you're gay."

I never thought of myself as gay. Rather, as having a bad habit particularly resistant to being broken. The Freudians attempted to bail out the sea of my guilt (that endless gray Puritan ocean); a behaviorist prescribed a rubber band around my wrist which I would snap when any "troublesome thoughts" surfaced.

"Well," I say, "my sons." I push a button and my bed rises up into a throne. "My kingdom shall be divided."

I give them a brief overview of the trusts and the guardians, the process of spending down. Medi-Medi, I explain, as Ms. O'Malley explained it to me. Given my foresight in applying for SSDI I have been Officially Disabled for more than the requisite twenty-four months, so Medicare has kicked in; and once I am asset-free, Medicaid will also. The details—for instance, that Charlie's birthright has been put into a trust with Dexter as trustee—I glide swiftly over. (I fear otherwise Charlie's portion might end up tossed to street children in Saigon—excuse me, Ho Chi Minh City— or donated to some foundation for the preservation of banana slugs.) The lawyer will go over the details with them tomorrow in his office at 10:00. The papers have been drawn up. The instruments will be signed and duly witnessed.

Dexter shakes my hand—shakes my hand!—and leaves.

I walk my elbows back along the white sheets, lower my torso. "You talk, Charlie."

Like Hamlet, he has undergone a sea change. No, he has not decided to follow his brother Dexter into public service.

But the whole trip was—well, a trip. He has gotten in touch with his heritage—not, you understand, Governor Bradford and his dour great-great-great-great-great grandfathers. His mother came from Main Line Philadelphia Quaker stock, and he has, with great enthusiasm, been reading about the early doings of Quaker founder George Fox. "Those guys were really radical, Dad," he says, growing so excited that he sprays me with a soft offering of his saliva. "Oops, sorry. You know what they used to do? They used to march through the streets naked. Through the streets of London. It was shocking because you couldn't tell people's rank—I mean nobody looked rich or poor when they were naked, they just looked—you know, like naked people. I mean, I'm descended from them."

He is going back beyond this, to the days when our forebears worshipped stocks and stones. He has discovered the pagan gods of Albion; the band is going to rename itself Magog after one of them. They will sing of a happier time when we all lived in huts of twigs and mud, with our goats and pigs and sheep wandering happily in and out of the manse.

Then he is silent. After a while he says: "Mom says, uh, she says hi."

"Tell her hi from me."

He sits there, studying the elongated tips of his fingers for so long that I wonder if he hasn't perhaps imbibed some illegal substance.

"Dad," he says. "Dad. Do you worry about the end? I mean, about really suffering?"

I find it slightly amusing that my son thinks this doesn't qualify as real suffering. I must wear it well.

"Because, Dad—I would do anything for you. If you

ever—wanted—anything—" and I understand he is volun-
teering to help me kill myself. "You know, Dad. You know."

I strove to break my son of the habit of saying 'you know.'
I am glad I did not succeed. I reach out and rub his shoulders. "Charlie," I say. "Charlie."

The Discharge Planner has done her work. Like pus oozing
from an orifice, like noxious effluent into the harbor, I have
been discharged—into a supported-living situation, a motel-like building that, although it is only a few years old, has
already begun to go to seed. I am taking classes to help me
adjust to my new state at an organization called Beacon for
the Blind. Even before I joined this elect company I found
the name a strange one—whatever did blind people want
with a beacon?

The Beacon for the Blind van drops me off at my apartment. In dim light the world has become a work of abstract
expressionism. (Bright light has become a work of pain.) I
sit down on the couch, covered with such cheap material
that even through my trousers it makes my flesh prickle. I
lean over and turn on the radio. "What sort of an effect do
you think this will have on Senator Barrows's career?" I must
admit that my heart leaps up—my brother in trouble! My
handsome, heterosexual brother! My brother the senator,
with his house five times the size of the one that had once
been mine! And then I remember Dexter's alliance. Or perhaps it is now a misalliance.

"Well," the commentator sounds vaguely amused. "I
don't think the problems that our state's other political dy-
nasty has been experiencing will make the public any more
tolerant of this situation. I think it's a lot more likely that

their reaction will be 'Enough is enough.' It's also safe to say that either of these problems coming alone might have been seen differently—but the fact that Senator Barrows seems to have left his son to struggle alone with quite a severe drug problem while he himself was off pursuing this—relationship . . ."

It turns out that my seventeen-year-old nephew, Joshua, was found in a hallway in Roxbury "suffering from an apparent drug overdose," in the words of the Boston Police. (I am no monster: the minute I hear this I feel guilty for my momentary thrill of joy.) His mother was unreachable, on a photo safari in Kenya; when Joshua came to, he gave the hospital staff, who had been unable to reach his father, a number where he could be contacted. His father was chauffeured to the hospital by a woman whom the tabloids will describe as "a voluptuous blond." An enterprising reporter jotted down her license number, tracked her down, interviewed her friends and neighbors: the scandal broke.

Four hundred years ago our ancestors would have been put in stocks or in the dunking chair. My sister-in-law is shown disembarking from a plane, looking grim and weary. Joshua enters a fancy drug treatment program, the senator's office issues a statement filled with "profound regret" and a plea to be allowed "to work with his wife and son to do all we can to heal the difficult situation in which we now find ourselves."

The press carries reports that his cousin had prostituted himself to support his drug habit. Dexter has himself photographed at a childcare center. Dexter has himself photographed coaching a youth hockey team in Dorchester. I learn that while Dexter does not believe that we can use volunteerism as a substitute for social programs which are both needed and cost-effective he believes that our society has become increasingly fragmented: we have an obligation to all work together for the common good. I am surprised Dexter is not shown in some similar pose with the AIDS-stricken. I had thought mine own afflictions would be "spun."

But no, Dexter patiently explains to me when he comes to visit me a week after my discharge: his campaign is aimed at the "demographics" that he hasn't got. He reports to me on the results of various focus groups that assure him that "the gays," as he puts it, will vote for him without his extending any particular nods in their direction, while the white working-class vote—

"Well, Dad, I didn't really come over here to talk to you about demographics and focus groups." Dexter is telling me that he is going to marry. He tells me his fiancée's name. I do not recognize it. I was not aware that he even had a steady girlfriend.

"Sure, sure," he is saying. Don't I remember—she came to the summerhouse a couple of years ago?

I remember a girl, broad-shouldered, big-boned, athletic, a trifle too hearty, given to guffawing at the dinner table, long red hair and freckles—the sort who will still look girlish at fifty. I remember that she and Dexter occupied separate bedrooms at a time when it was tacitly agreed that no concessions to propriety were needed.

"Has she been your girlfriend all this time?"

"No. We've been friends for a long time. I think it's not bad groundwork."

He would like, he is telling me, to move into the flat I

have left empty in Louisburg Square. Of course, I tell him. Dexter will bed his bride in the same room in which I, on rare occasion, bedded his mother. He will walk in scuffed brown leather slippers down the uneven, charming front steps to retrieve the morning papers which landed in the bushes, as once I walked in scuffed brown leather slippers.

"Is this on account of Rob's shenanigans?"

"It moved the timetable along a little bit."

This is how we know the truth in our family: you take what is said and move it a few degrees to the left. So my son will enter a marriage—"loveless" sounds too harsh, although there will be no love there—a marriage of affection, a convenient arrangement. He will follow in his father's footsteps.

Charlie arrives at my door with an offering of fresh-baked whole wheat bread. "I made you one myself but it came out kind of like a brick. So I bought you this at the Zen bakery."

"Thank you, Charlie," I say. When I was sighted, I would have called this action I now make "fumbling"; now I understand that I am searching the air for the proffered loaf.

Dexter thinks a brilliant doctor could cure me; Charlie thinks whole wheat bread and Chinese herbs could cure me. Despair is a meal you eat alone.

But I share the Zen loaf with Charlie, nibbling on my portion: I'm afraid of what whole wheat bread will do to my fragile digestive system.

"Dad, this place—it must depress you."

"It's—" I want to say something clever, but I have nothing clever to say. "Yes," I say. "Yes."

"Don't you want some art to hang on the walls? I could ask Mom—that Jasper Johns print, you really loved that—"

How Patricia and I had rowed over that when we split apart! Our twenty-five-year marriage may have been a sham in some ways but, as that junior professor at Harvard who wasn't given tenure taught me, bourgeois marriage is primarily an economic arrangement. How we had fought over the spoils. Recently diagnosed, knowing I would soon, too soon, leave this world of things forever, how I had clung to every molecule I possessed. And our convenient marriage, our rational marriage, our placid marriage turned into an orgy of smashed crystal and slammed doors. I'd screamed words that I couldn't have imagined coming out of my mouth: "You ugly bitch! You ugly dog-faced bitch!" Once I'd called her that she was free to scream, "You faggot! You fucking little cocksucker!" And then I was free to come back with something even crueler; and then she was free, etc. Was it exhaustion that finally made us abandon the battle? Or fear of how much further we might go?

"I couldn't see it well enough, Charlie."

"Really, Dad?"

"Really, Charlie." How well could I see it? If I put my face a few inches from it, I could see an inch or two of color, which would no doubt awake in me the memory of the whole . . . I don't want to tell Charlie how flimsy, from where I am now standing, all the things of this life are. Those things, those things! The cars and country houses and charming hand-painted three-footed teapots bought at the Paris flea market, the first edition of *To the Lighthouse*, the old Billie Holiday 78s, the antique weather vane, the quilt my great-great-grandmother sewed . . .

My watch beeps. "Time for my Acilovar," I say.

A month has passed. I am back in the hospital again. A

stubborn respiratory infection. "I'm not pessimistic," the pulmonologist says. "I wouldn't panic on this one." (Will they ever say: "I'd panic on this one"?)

I am shaking when Ms. Brenda A. O'Malley enters; she asks me if I am cold.

"I'm scared."

"What are you scared of?"

"Death."

I meant to say it with a certain ironic flip, but I didn't quite pull it off. Suddenly, there death is—not a man in a black hood from a Bergman movie, not a Day of the Dead figurine brought back from Mexico—but my death, my very own death, my one and only death—hunched naked in the air between us.

"Yes," she says, and nods.

I hate her. I want to hit her. (For the record, I have never hit a woman. I have hit my son Dexter once, my son Charlie more than once, I am ashamed to say.) I hate dear Ms. Brenda A. O'Malley because she does not take thirty-seven pills a day, because she has no lesions on her skin, no lesions in her brain. I hate her for loving me; because I do think that for a few seconds after I said the word "death" she did love me, as momentarily and intensely as I hated her.

And then: she looks down, smoothes her skirt. We are like two strangers who had coupled in some anonymous dark corner.

"You're kind," I say. "You're very kind. I want you to go away."

"Shall I come back later?" she asks.

I am not kind. I say, "No. Just go away."

Forgive and forget: that is our motto here on Ward 14B. Did

liquid shit pour out of you onto the floor in the hallway yesterday? Did you awake screaming in the night? Lose your balance while tottering down the hall and trip over someone's roving IV pole, ripping the needle from his arm? No problem. Did you tell nice Brenda A. O'Malley, MSW, to go away? Why, no hard feelings. She's back again the next morning, smiling, swishing into your room in her silk skirt that rustles against itself.

I sign a form. I understand that these drugs are experimental; side effects that have been reported so far include nausea, dizziness, fatigue, anemia (may be severe), gastrointestinal distress, diarrhea, vomiting . . .

The doctor comes in again. Up, he says. Down. Elevated. Normal. A certain medication seems to be working: not, you understand, on the root of the problem, but on one of the more irritating symptoms.

Up, he says. Down. 57. 310. 17. 17. 18. When it gets up to 24 I can go home. Home to my motel-like apartment. 19. 21. A dip down to 18. 22. 23. 27. You're out.

It is Charlie who escorts me home, driving my BMW. I take his arm as we go into my living facility.

"Dad," he says when I am ensconced on the cheap couch. "Something kind of weird happened yesterday."

"Yes, son?" I say.

"Well, it's about the money, your money—"

"My former assets—"

"Yeah, whatever. I, uh, I, uh . . . I was going to buy you this sculpture. From Jake's gallery. On Beacon Street. I thought, uh—you know, something you could touch. It's kind of—Donatello. A lot of texture. I remember how much you liked the Donatellos when we were in Florence—"

"That's kind of you, Charlie, but—"

"You know, so I called Dexter, you know—"

"Yes," I say, "I know Dexter."

"Sorry. I had to get his permission, on account of him being the trustee."

"You are only twenty, Charlie."

"He said no."

"I'm glad he did. I wouldn't want you spending your money."

"I don't want the money, Dad. The way I live, I'm happy. We kind of got in a fight. Dexter and I. And I ended up calling the bank and then I talked to the lawyer. It's all gone, Dad."

"What do you mean?"

"My money. Your money, the part of it that was supposed to be for me. I called Dexter back. He said he'd had trouble raising money—he said it was just a temporary cash flow thing. Because of Rob's—you know. Sorry."

"What?" I say. "What?"

I am free, I am frail, I am light as the wind. I am a scrap of man. I have nothing.

"Charlie," I say, and reach for his hand. It is not where I expected it to be, and rather than searching the air for it I withdraw.

The next morning I call Dexter. I leave a message on his answering machine. I leave a message with his secretary at Burton, Myers & Dudley. I leave a message at his campaign headquarters.

He does not return my calls.

I go to see my doctor. I have lost another three pounds. I go to my class at Beacon for the Blind. I listen over and over again to a single cut on a CD, Maria Callas singing *Ombra leggiera*. I leave my daily round of messages for Dexter.

Charlie invites me for dinner at the run-down house in Somerville he and some of his friends have rented. I'll like his new place, he tells me: it's cool. A sort of hippie commune, I gather, although they themselves would not use those words to describe it.

I must confess, I don't find this place cool: rather, seedy and depressing, and not at all clean: I am frightened I will catch something. Charlie has gotten over his embarrassment about my state; now he shows me off. "Hey, Gerald," he says to a friend of one of his housemates. "This is my father. He's got AIDS."

"A pleasure to meet you, Gerald," I say.

"Hey," says Gerald. "Cool shades."

Sitting in this house—my goodness, how many of these shaggy youths who straggle through the living room actually reside here?—reminds me a bit of visiting the New England Aquarium. I am the observer: these strange creatures are the ones behind glass. Not strange, mark you, on account of their leopard print hair and their sundry pierced body parts. Look at this one, entering the front door, tiptoeing in on his Rollerblades —who can imagine having a body so obedient to one's commands? And look how they simply plunk themselves down in a chair without giving it a second thought: no arranging of joints, no consideration of balance. One minute they're standing up, then they're sitting down, then they're up again! Amazing!

When I rise, what an enormous number of calculations I have to perform. Once I was like them. Once I, too, was twenty and healthy and did not perform these tender, elaborate computations. Once I was uncalculating.

Ten of us sit down at table. The dish we have eaten, I am informed when we are nearly done with our dinner, is called Dumpster Ratatouille. Yes, my son, out of his ecological principles, scavenges what others have discarded. He is not, he hastens to assure me, in competition with the others who are neither reapers nor sowers, the genuine and official Homeless. Having no kitchens, no cast-iron frying pans, no cutting boards, they pass up the soft green peppers, the tomatoes with a shopper's thumbprint in them.

After dinner we drink spiced tea, and one by one they drift away—to night jobs at Kinko's, to movies showing at dingy repertory houses, upstairs to read or listen to their stereos or make love. Only Charlie and I are left.

"I've been trying to call Dexter," I confess. "I've been calling him, but he hasn't—"

"I really wanted to buy that statue for you, Dad."

"No, Charlie, but—"

"I really wanted to."

"It's just that I'm so tired," I say.

"Are you too tired to go home? Do you want to stay here?"

I had meant I was tired in a much more general way, but suddenly I want nothing more than to sleep—to sleep now, to sleep here.

"Just for tonight."

"You can sleep in my bed."

"Tonight," I say to Charlie. "Just tonight. I'm tired. I'm just tired."

"Do you want to go to bed now?" he asks.

But when he leads me to his room and I sit down on his bed, the sheets are gritty to my touch. "Would you mind," I say, "terribly? Changing the sheets . . ."

"Sure, Dad," he says. I stand gingerly up, and he yanks at the sheet, reeling it in toward him like a fisherman his net.

He disappears down the hallway, then returns.

"Hey, Dad, you got any quarters?"

"Charlie?"

"For the Laundromat."

"Oh, don't—" I say. "Don't you have a spare sheet?"

"It's cool," he says. "The Laundromat's not far."

I reach into my pocket and feel for quarters. Quarters are easy.

"Is this enough?" I haven't done laundry in a public Laundromat since that summer on the Cape.

"Yeah, Dad. It's great. You going to be okay? It'll take me about an hour and a half."

"I'm fine," I say.

"I could bring the boom box in here. I have some opera CDs. Well, one, I think—"

"No," I say. "I'll just rest."

"You sure, Dad?"

"I'm sure."

I curl up like a fetus on the bare blue and white mattress ticking, my head on the naked white pillow, which for some reason has the word *Pillow* repeated over and over again on it in letters several inches high.

I do not drift off to sleep. Drifting is something that happened in that other world. Here fatigue wars with pain which wars with a restless feeling in my legs.

At some point Charlie returns, shakes me awake, leads me to a chair, makes the bed. Then he unbuttons the buttons of my shirt, kneels at my feet and unlaces my shoes, pulls my feet free, tugs off my socks. He leaves my trousers on and takes me back to bed.

When I wake up in the morning a breathing blue blur is lying on the uncarpeted floor next to me. I can just make out unkempt hair rising like a halo around a head. I smell his smell.

"Charlie," I whisper. "Charlie. Are you there? Charlie?"

He grunts. "Dad," he mumbles. "Dad."

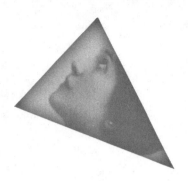

Goliath

The scrivener smoothes the damp clay. With his stylus he presses down the call to the face-off: "Valley of Elah, Exit 27 off the Beersheba-Shiloh Freeway. The day after the first full moon in Kislev. Mark ye this number: 24. Later. P.S. Ye are toast."

Men whose breath smells of wine and herbs clap Goliath on the back and roar, "24, man. Fucking 24!"

"We're counting on you, boy!"

"24!" they whoop.

Not a wineshop in Gath but they're saying, "What's your pleasure? Wine or barley-brew?" Once disgrace was Goliath's meat and shame his wine. Now Goliath doesn't go out without his brothers, who like him are possessors of supernumerary digits, so that the number of their fingers and toes totals twenty-four, but unlike him having an ordinary height of three and a half cubits: his posse to protect him from the force of wild love.

"24, man, fucking 24!"

"Those goddamn sons of Abraham won't know what hit them."

Goliath can't stop a goofy grin from spreading over his face.

"Next one's on me!" shouts another voice from the dark cave of a bar.

His brother Lahmi says, "Neither wine nor brew shall pass his lips till the battle hath been joined and won." Truth: the wine and brew make the headaches worse, but if Goliath says, "I am sore and aching. A thumping is in my head and the very jointures of my body swell and offend me"—well, then it's just: "Brother, what you need is a good fornication!" "I know a wanton you could lie with carnally," "Corruption, lad, corruption—we all have need of it."

Lahmi hoists himself up onto a table and puts both his hands on his brother's shoulders. "Let not his might run out of him, like a spring-river overflowing its banks. He shall make his strength safe and fast, until after our enemies have been smited. When their blood waters the grasses of the Valley of Elah, then shall my brother's seed flow out from him."

Once Goliath was a boy like any other boy: scampering with his brothers and cousins out of the city gates when they were opened to let a caravan in, feasting on the wild grapes and honey they gathered in the wilderness, throwing rocks at the soldiers guarding the checkpoints. One day they had even ventured to the chain-link fence topped with coiled razor wire and hung with metal signs inscribed with runes none could any longer decode. In the unpruned trees beyond the fence they saw the fluttering remnants of torn plastic carrier bags hanging like moss in the trees.

A wailing hermit, barefooted and white-bearded, patrolling the perimeter of the fence came toward them. The hermit's fingernails were long and yellowed, mottled like the horn of some beast: "The tale has been told to me," he wailed, "and I will tell it to thee, how this place came to be a wasteland giving birth to naught but death: A beast of the air—some scorned god, mayhaps, or demon—rained upon the cities of the plain fire and brimstone. The people within those cities became in a flash naught but shadows." The hermit wept as he spake these words and, weeping still, continued on his way. He turned and called back to them: "Stay away, my lads, stay well away. Megadeath! Megamegadeath!"

Goliath grew. At first his growth was measured in mere digits and palms: with pride he felt himself to be gaining in stature, leaving his boyhood behind. But he grew and grew. First he towered over his elder brothers by a single cubit, then by two. From an ordinary boy whom the elders could not always tell apart from his brothers and cousins, he became singular: the one, the only Goliath. He was taunted in the streets: "Fee-Fie-Fo-Fum," the children called after him. "Fee-Fi-Fo-Fum."

War looms, and everything changes: the endless 24/7, day in, day out, same old, same old; the whole Monday-nothing, Tuesday-nothing, Wednesday-and-Thursday-nothing, Friday-for-a-change-a-little-more-nothing, Saturday-and-Sunday-nothing thing flies away. No longer do the men of Gath tremble before death: they rush to meet it, eager to be tested like metal in the fire. It seems the events of their lives, which heretofore have been a mere collection of haphazard incidents, now form themselves into a coherent narrative. The Philistines look back over their own lives and their life as a people: the course of it has been leading inexorably to zero hour in the Valley of Elah.

Pain wakes Goliath. He works his mouth open and shut, twisting it around, unkinking it. He cups his hands around his jaw and rubs. The surfeit of growth hormone that causes giantism results in overgrowth of the bone and temporo-mandibular joint pain.

It's not just his jaw that aches: the very sinews and join-ings of his body do. The shin bone's connected to the knee bone, the knee bone's connected to the thigh bone, the thigh bone's connected to the hip bone, etc., and he is aware of ev-ery one of those bonds.

Sometimes when he wakes in the night, Goliath feels an overarching tenderness for his body. He imagines that be-yond the hills of Judea or past the Negev Desert there is a tribe of beings so colossal that the women of that race could scoop him up in their arms, cradle him like a baby, rub away his pains with ointments of camphor and myrrh and some magical substance of which only they have knowledge.

His brothers, sprawled around him on the portico, breathe heavily. That sound mingles with the snuffles and sighs from the sheep and goats in the pens of the adjacent yard. Goliath clambers to his feet, and, crouching almost double, passes through the doorway into the house, threading his way across the sleeping forms of other brothers and cousins who during the night migrated into the house from the garden.

Peoples of the desert are scavengers, and scavengers are wanderers, following water and the promise of water, budging their flocks of sheep and goats before them, seeking forage and scrub, moving from the harvest in the olive groves to tend the terraced hillsides where barley is grown. Inside the houses of their villages they are not still, not even at night: they may fall asleep in the gardens at the core of their houses and then in the middle of the night make their way to the roofs or stretch out upon carpets laid on the inner floors of packed earth.

He hears, from the women's quarters above, the sound of his sister Asthah's slow and steady rocking, matched by her slow and steady mumbling: "Caleb, Judah, Arba, Hebron, Anak, Sheshai, Ahiman, Talmai, Debir, Kirjath-sepher Othniel Kenaz. Caleb." She says again, "Caleb, Caleb" and whispers out a hollow laugh.

At first when she came back from captivity, every member of the household—old and young, master and servant, male and female—was kept awake by her ceaseless chanting of the names of cities and towns, kings and gods, the naming of the lines laid across this land. Now her babble has become part of the fabric of their lives.

He steps outside into the moonless night. He hears the chirp of crickets. The stars press close and closer; it seems they might leave their firmament behind and descend down to this earthly realm. He hears the sound of cartwheels rumbling against cobblestones: no doubt some scavenger seeking discarded wine jugs. The night world of Gath belongs to those who glean in the dumpsters, the eaters of parched corn, the harlots and the vagabonds.

"Hey, big boy."

He answers not.

The wanton draws closer to him; the musky scent of attar of roses fills his nostrils.

"Don't be shy." Her lips so close the words are lambent upon his ear. She strokes a single finger down the ridge of his collarbone.

He shakes himself free of her touch. "Gold have I not; silver neither."

"Neither gold nor silver do I seek. Only the pleasure of lying with you."

"You think I have forgot who you are. I know you, and I know your name. Japar. Not long ago you mocked me."

"'Tis ancient history."

"I am at once far more a man than any other man and far less. You said my thing was like the budded rose of a child."

"That was then, and this is now."

He shows to her his broad back.

"You think we harlots are weak-willed?" she says, massaging his shoulders as she speaks. Her touch soothes his aching joints. "It is no easy thing to be a woman such as I, in this new world of the patriarchs. I shall not easily surrender my desire for you."

"Now you desire me . . ."

"We all live within these city walls," she says, her hands kneading deep within the muscles of his shoulder. "You like this, do you not? True enough, once I mocked you, as all once did. But now thou art no longer scorned and pilloried; now thou art raised up and praised above all men."

"Your hands soothe the aching within me."

"The night is deep and velvet dark. No one will see us. We can join together in whatever fashion pleaseth us both."

Seeing that he hesitates still, she adds, "Our pleasures shall be manifold. We may sate ourselves not in some grunting act of copulation but in a manner more cunning and more subtle. And in addition to the fleshly pleasures that our joining brings, on the morrow I shall have the pleasure of bragging that I have lain with Goliath, that I have borne our hero's great weight. And you—you may glory in taking the one who once derided you."

She takes his hand and leads him toward the room where she abides, beyond the souk, far from the decent quarters of the town. He pads after her like an overgrown puppy, watching her haunches ripple beneath the fine linen of her gown, drawing in the musky smell wafting after her.

Shortly after Asthah and the others left alive returned, a delegation of women from the tribe of Ruth came down from the hills. The elders barred the city gates against them. The women veiled themselves in white and chanted, clapping in rhythmic time, turning now to the right, now to the left: "Isis/Astarte/Diana/Hecate/Demeter/ . . . Kali/Demeter/Hecate/Diana/Astarte/Isis . . . Our goddess gave birth to your god."

The young men mounted the ramparts of the city walls and hiked up their robes, showing their bare backsides.

The women shouted, one after another: "Do you think such a sight strikes fear in our hearts?" "Were you not born of woman?" "Have not we women given birth to you men?" "Have we not wiped clean such butts a million times?" "Nay, a million multiplied by a million times?"

"Get thee hence!" the men called down.

One of the men lifted a bullhorn to his lips and called out, "What was the first plague visited upon our people?"

"Laser-guided missiles!" the other men chorused back.

"And the second plague?"

"Apache helicopters!"

"And the next plague?"

"Kalashnikovs!"

"And the next?"

"Sidewinders!"

"And?"

"Arrowheads!"

"Hydra rockets!"

"Scuds!"

"And the next plague?"

"F-16s!"

"And the last plague, the worst plague of all?"

"The last plague, the worst plague of all: the plague of feminists!"

It was said that at night a few of the women who had returned from captivity made their way—whether of their own volition or thrust out by their families—to join Ruth's people beyond the walls of the city.

The next night Goliath awakens again. He lies still upon the carpet spread upon the earth, staring up at the moon, a newborn's fingernail. He hears Asthah's whispered chanting: ". . . from the shore of the salt sea, from the bay that looketh southward, to Maaleh-acrabbim, along to Zin."

He looks to his left: she is hunkered on the ground next to him, her eyes fixed intently on him.

She smiles when she sees him, although she does not cease to speak: "And the fenced cities are Ziddim, Zer, and Hammath, Rakkath, and Chinnereth and . . ."

"Hush," he whispers, "hush."

He stretches out his hand to her, and she takes it. When she first came back she could not abide the touch of any man, not even him.

"Sister, why do you watch over me so?"

"These are the dukes that came of the Horites . . . I did not join the women of Ruth . . . Duke Lotan, Duke Shobal, Duke Zibeon . . . they spoke of healing and I . . . Duke Anah, Duke Dishon, Duke Ezer, Duke Dishan . . . I would that I could drink their blood . . . and Bela the son of Beor reigned in Edom: and the name of his city was Dinhabah . . . a cup of it would I drain to its very dregs . . . And Bela died, and Jobab the son of Zerah of Bozrah reigned in his stead . . ."

"If it is what thou truly desires, I will hang an Israelite by his toes and let his blood drain from him and bring it back to thee."

"And Jobab died, and Husham of the land of Temani reigned in his stead . . . I would there could be justice. . . . And Husham died, and Hadad the son of Bedad, who smote Midian in the field of Moab, reigned in his stead: and the name of his city was Avith . . . vengeance is a poor second . . . And Hadad died, and Samlah of Masrekah reigned in his stead . . . Yet the poor second must I take . . . and Samlah died, and Saul of Rehboth by the river reigned in his stead . . . My hatred sickens me . . . And Baal-hanan the son of Achbor died . . . to lust for blood . . . and Hadar reigned in his stead . . . yet I can no more will myself free of it . . . and the name of his city was Pau . . . then will the stars from the sky . . ."

"Sister, would it soothe you to walk outside beneath the stars?"

Her only answer is the slipping of her thin hand into his paw.

The night is silent save for her whispering, "Pharez begat Hezron / And Hezron begat Ram . . ." Each time she says "begat" her voice lilts upward as if she were puzzled.

In the midst of her chant a single word rises like a bubble in water: "Stars." And then she continues, ". . . Amminadab / And Amminadab begat? Nahshon / and—stars—"

"The stars?" Goliath asks. "The stars are beautiful?"

"Yes, yes," she mutters, then hurries on, "and Ram begat Amminadab / And Amminadab begat Nahshon / and Nahshon . . ."

Her shift has slipped down off her shoulder and he glimpses her breast, which could be the breast of any other girl on the verge of womanhood. Her experiences have not marked her; her body has swallowed up within itself all evidence.

Goliath imagines his foot crushing a grizzled face that might have belonged to one of her captors; he imagines entering the soldiers they will defeat not with his own member but with a stick or a spear.

"Hush," he says.

Asthah is silent but rocks back and forth in agitation. Shortly a plea bursts out of her mouth: "Oh, brother, let me say my words again. When they do not issue forth, they dam up inside me. They clot in my mouth."

"If silence pains you, you must speak."

She furrows her brow, taps the air with her left index finger. "Nahshon, Nahshon, yes, Nahshon. Nahshon begat Salmon / And Salmon begat Boaz, and Boaz begat Obed. Issue have I none. I beget naught but these begats." She spits these last two sentences into the void that would usually be a pause for the drawing in of breath. "Obed begat Jesse, and Jesse begat David."

She leans her head against him, not ceasing her muttering. A night breeze blows the scent of olives from the groves on the hillside above the city.

At last he speaks the words he has been intending for the past hour to utter: "Last night—I knew a woman for the first time."

He feels her body grow tense, her chanting becoming more frantic. "Caleb, Judah, Arba—Kind?—Hebron, Anak, Sheshai, Ahiman, Talmai—thought you of me?—Debir—"

"As the ether that surrounds us are my thoughts of you."

"Pain?"

"Knowledge had I of her, and there is no knowledge without pain," Goliath says, but he sees he has not answered her question in saying this.

When Asthah's physical wounds had healed they took her to the witch doctor. Asthah wailed when a dove was sacrificed so its entrails could be read. The healer steepled his fingers and said to the family: "Post-traumatic stress disorder hath triggered an underlying psychosis . . . Go ye to the herbalist and she will give unto thine child an infusion which may alleviate some symptoms." He raised his gaze and met that of Asthah's father: "Hereafter will she be mad, even unto the hour of her death."

They led her home and shut her up safely in the women's quarters.

Goliath's pain is not the only secret kept locked within the walls of this house. Better she should have been returned to them a corpse, a martyr safe in the ground, than this living reminder of their humiliation.

The king speaks, and his tribunes and spin doctors and minions sit in the square underneath the date palms alongside the gurgling spring and relay what he has said: "Evil must be purged from our world. If the tribes of this land join not with us, we will make our way alone—for are we not the Philistines, great lovers of freedom and defenders of liberty? Yet the Canaanites are now yoked with us, and the Hittites, and Amorites, and Perizzites, and Hivites—even the Jebusites are getting with the program."

In the distance dust is being raised by the grunts drilling on the plateaus in the hills above Gath. The sound of their chants fades in and out of earshot of those gathered in the square: " Left-right-left / left-right-left / keep ye in step . . ." "All the tribes of the world," the minions continue, "cry out against the crimes of the Israelites. Did not Joshua son of Nun cause the walls of Jericho to tumble down, and then did he not utterly destroy all that was in the city, both man and woman, young and old, and ox, and sheep, and ass and then, add ignominy to horror, torching the corpses of man and beast alike? Did he not then, unashamed, proclaim these deeds to all the world, and say that his god had commanded him to do this? And did not their Samson carry out his suicide mission, bringing down the pillars and the roof above, a mass murderer of innocents?"

"Left-right-left / left-right-left . . ." is carried by the winds coming down out of the hills.

A chariot with a bumper sticker that says "NUKE SAMMY" whips past.

Spray-painted in red paint on an adobe wall are the words GOLIATH IS NOT THE ANSWER. A spray-painted x is splayed

across it, with the words next to it: IF YOU AREN'T FOR THE
HOME TEAM, GET OUT OF THE STADIUM.

The town crier, making his circuit, calls out: "The shadow of the sundial stands at its most paltry: noon is nigh. The
king is in his palace; Dagon in his temple; all is well.

"Weather here in Gath: the sun shineth above us, and
sweet rain will fall tonight. Weather in the Vale of Elah: current temperature—16 degrees centigrade, with precipitation.
Yet take heart, fellow Philistines, for the casting of sticks this
morning by the prognosticators reveal there shall be blue
skies and bright sun on game day!"

Toward dusk the warriors troop down from training in
the hills. Their faces are streaked with dirt and sweat so their
eyes glisten like black jewels.

A beardless youth rushes to Goliath's house. "Quickly come!
The co hath need of thee."

His mother calls to Asthah, "A clean linen tunic! Kohl for
his eyes! Aye, brothers too give hand. Perfumed oils!" She
claps her hands once, twice, thrice: "Apace! Apace!"

"Yet nine days remain until the battle is to be joined,"
Goliath says, lumbering to his feet. "The armies of Israel—
have they attacked?"

"No, no, fear not—" says the messenger.

"My son knows not the meaning of the word fear."

Goliath stares into his mother's eyes, which give him no
signal of complicity, only her shining belief in him.

"All the foot soldiers," gasps out the messenger, "are called
together, arrayed in order in their brigades and their mani-
ples. The light armored vehicles draw nigh into the square,
the pommelers are called for, also the spear-carriers and the

axmen and the javeliners and the thrusters of pikes. Thou must shew thyself to the armies of our king, that they shall have the sweet foretaste of victory."

As Goliath approaches the center of the city, a brother on either side of him, he smells the sweet water of the spring, the scent of dates in the air, mixed with the smell of dust raised by a thousand tromping feet and hears a drill instructor bellowing at one of the recruits: "Once thou wast regarded as an insect, but now it is evident that thou art less than that: a maggot. Dost thou admit thou art a maggot?"

"Sire, yes, sire."

"Say it, soldier."

"I am a maggot, sire."

"Louder, damsel—"

Espying Goliath, the drill sergeant turns his attention to all the men of his company: "Ah, pray silence, for comes before us now a man who crawleth not on his belly like the spawn of some slug, but a man whose grasp doth graze the very heavens . . . the one, the only: Goliath!"

Goliath breaks his stride; looks abashed at all the huzzahs and alarums, but his Sergeant-York-aw-gee-shucks manner just makes the crowd exult the more.

Now the overlord strides in front of the assembly, pulls himself up to his full height, adjusts the folds of his robe, and says, "Men, looking out upon you, I see arrayed before me the finest pommels and javelins and chariots and light armored vehicles in all the Fertile Crescent." Here he pauses for the cheers, which duly come. "Yet it is not with these pommels and these javelins and chariots and light armored vehicles that the victory shall be ours."

Goliath hears his name, spoken by a single voice within the crowd then taken up in general: "Goliath! Goliath! Goliath!"

The commander lets them get pumped up for a while, then raises both his arms next to his head and gestures for silence.

"Human factors. Human factors. That shall the battle decide."

"And the greatest of the human factors," calls out a voice from the crowd, "Goliath!"

"Goliath! Goliath! Goliath!"

"Get up here, boy!" the overlord says.

The hurrahs ricochet inside Goliath's head. He wonders what would happen if he were to clap his hands over his ears, hunker down into a squat, rock from side to side, shouting, "Cease! Cease forthwith!" But only wonders.

"When they see our Goliath, then shall they turn tail and run. For his presence shall strike more fear into their hearts than any of our missiles which seeketh heat or our daisy cutters; yea, even more than the sight of our stealth bombers in the sky. But then, my men, it must be your duty to turn this rout into a cleansing: we must purge this evil from our world forevermore."

Still they chant his name.

The moon is no longer a Turkish crescent. The moon waxes; Goliath's fear waxes with it. He eats the bread of cowardice alone: it is dry and sticks in his craw. He knows full well what the Israelites will do should they take him captive: double payback for what the Philistines did to Samson. They will devise some torment that makes having eyes gouged out, being bound in fetters of brass and forced to turn a grindstone in an unending circuit—a human, eyeless mule—make that look enviable.

That night Goliath watches the waxing moon above the hills of Judea. The next night it has crossed some boundary so now it can be said to be swollen, like a hunchback or a pregnant woman. Just days now.

Asthah finds him in the garden, running his fingernail down a shaft of grass, splitting it in half.

She lays her hand on his shoulder; he shakes it off, clambers to his feet, paces. (Her frantic speech continues all the while: "The king of Jericho; the king of Ai; the king of Jerusalem; the king of Hebron; the king of Jarmuth . . .")

"Pray, silence, sister dear."

She lowers her voice, but does not cease to speak. ". . . the king of Gezer; the king of Debir . . . I seek to wear out these words, as a cloth is worn to tatters by usage . . . the king of Arad; the king of Libnah . . . I love you. . . . Kedesh, Gaza, Goshen . . . As I never have . . . Moab, Kadesh, Golan . . . and never will another . . ."

"I would it were the day of battle. I cannot abide this waiting."

"Gilid, Gilgal . . . in the hills . . . Lebanon, Manasseh . . . the first rain hath . . . Jabbok, Bashan . . ."

Goliath speaks for her: "The first rain has fallen?"

"Yea . . . Bene-berak, Jahaz, Seir . . . walk outside the gates? . . . Mizpeh, Jahaz, Bene-berak . . ."

"To walk out in the hills and see the infant grasses that blanket the hillsides, just arisen after the first rains?"

"Yes! Yes! . . . Gilid, Gilgal, Lebanon, Manasseh . . ."

"I fear to leave the safety of the gates of this city. For whilst we tarried in the hills, unmindful and distracted, might not some stranger waylay us? For who would not gloat to say that they have felled the Philistines' giant?"

"These are the names of Esau's sons . . . Flee . . . Eliphaz the son of Adah the wife of Esau . . . Hie into the hills . . . Reuel the son of Bashemath the wife of Esau . . . I with thee . . . and the sons of Eliphaz were Teman, Omar, Sepho, and Gatam, and Kenaz . . ."

"How would we then live? Thou knowest what a poor, poor specimen of a man am I. My strength is no match for my vastness: I can neither plow nor sow a field, nor can I trot alongside of goats or sheep. I suppose I might exhibit myself to those who would, in terror of me, push toward me a plate of victuals or a jug of wine, and plead that I, in recompense of these offerings, depart and harry them no more? We are trapped within these walls of Gath, and trapped would we be without them."

"These are the dukes that came of the Horites, Duke Lotan, Duke Shobal, Duke Zibeon . . . locusts and wild honey . . . Duke Anah /Duke Dishon, Duke Ezer, Duke Dishan . . . our bread could be . . . And these the kings: Bela son of Beor reigned in Edom . . . water our wine . . ."

He cannot say to her: My hatred for the enemy seizes me more fiercely than lust for a woman ever has. I long to see their skulls cracked open, the soft jelly of their brains oozing onto the earth, as a jackal's jaw spills the slime from a bird's egg upon the ground. I long to hear the wails of their mothers, as even a mother hawk, returning to her nest to find it ravaged, her never-born fledglings fodder for some fox, keens as pitifully as any dove.

I could speak, sister, and I could say many words, but those words would be like the words you chant. My language is like a flock of birds that rises up from some outcropping and flies away, disappearing into the infinite sky. And what they would leave behind is the stone upon which they roosted, dark and motionless: the black rock of my hatred.

Then, at last, the terrible waiting for the day of battle is coming to an end: the moon is one night shy of full. The soldiers gather in marching order and set out to the patriotic shouts (and muffled sobs) of the women and the men too young or old for battle. Goliath, in a tumbrel surrounded by his brothers, is the last to go.

Soon they are arrived at the mountaintop where the armies of the Philistines are encamped, opposite the mountaintop where the armies of the Israelites are encamped. He finds at the very forefront of the bivouac a tent of gargantuan proportions for him to therein lodge—an omen unto the enemy.

He ambles toward the tent, but the morale officer and his crew stop him and say, "Not yet, brother. Not yet."

One of the crew adds, "For fear, like desire, is always about the event which has not yet occurred."

"College boy," says the morale officer, and claps his subaltern fondly on the back. "Hold fast, Goliath, let you show yourself in the sliver of time between dusk and darkness. Let the sight of you beget fear in them, and then their night shall be a confinement in which that fear shall swell and grow like a babe in its mother's womb."

And so he waits, seated at a trestle table at the front of the improvised mess, devouring the food put in front of him: mutton, squab, figs, olives, loaves of bread, pomegranate juice mixed with honey and water, goat, a vast pottage of barley. The mess hall grows quieter and quieter and then quiet. Goliath is licking goat grease from his fingers when he notices the absence of talk, hearing nothing but the chirping of crickets and the wind rustling the leaves of the olive trees in the groves below them.

And he sees that they are watching him attempting to fill the gorge within him. He surveys the mound of olive pits, the ribs of goat and sheep, the bowls scraped almost clean with the edge of his spoon. Yet he hungers still.

He turns his head away in shame.

But then he hears a single voice crying out, "Goliath!"

And then the chant becomes general: "Go-li-ath! Go-li-ath!" They clap their hands and stamp their feet upon the earth in rhythmic time, and his brothers urge him to his feet, put a jug of wine in each of his hands.

"Go-li-ath! Go-li-ath!"

"Down 'em, bro. Down 'em."

He sets first one then the other jug on the table. If he were to walk down this mountaintop, walk north, might he not live a life in the desert? Slay with his hands the wild beasts—lions and bears and crocodiles—all other men fear; or perhaps pluck locusts and doves from the air? His bones would ache from sleeping in the open; loneliness would be his lot, but might it not be better than this?

Lahmi fixes his eyes on him. The eyes of his brother are like the eyes of Asthah; they are like his own eyes. If Samuel's army routs the Philistines, what fate will befall them?

He hoists a jug into the air, chugalugs the wine, repeats the action with the other jug.

"Goliath! Goliath! Goliath!"

Lahmi hands him another jug of wine, and then another, and then another.

A Bedouin, acting as a spy for the Philistines, comes to their encampment and is led into the king's tent.

"Of the giant they have word, and the more they whisper about him, the more his height increases. From six cubits to eight to nine: now the common soldiers say he is the very image of the colossus which bestrides the harbor at Rhodes.

"Their morale office brought in a doctor from U. of Bethlehem who delivered unto them a lecture in which he spoke much of the excess of growth hormone which causeth giantism resulting in carpal tunnel syndrome, hypogonadism, lethargy, male lactation, cardiomyopathy—but afterward I heard the soldiers aver to one another that it was all just so much BS to keep them from deserting.

"Another rumor hath gone round—started, I believe, by the brass when the lecture by the physician failed to soothe the men—that Goliath is not a man at all but a form of wood or wicker, clothed like a man and animated by guy wires and pulleys and levers. But in response to this the common troops doth say: If they have the cleverness to create such a thing, which walketh and talketh and moveth like a man, had we not best fear them, and fear them sorely—for verily what other sorts of weapons might they have?"

Goliath spins from all the wine. How sweet this addled dullness! He gets led to the front of the encampment, paraded back and forth, men of normal height walking next to him.

He sees the watch fires in the opposite valley flickering on the faces of his enemy.

Full night descends; he half staggers, is half carried to his tent. In and out of drunken sleep he hears the women camp followers playing psaltery, tabouret, pipe, and harp, their songs at times elegies for those who have fallen in battles past, at other times taunts directed at the opposite mountain: *Our slaves were you once, and again will be . . . Our god's greater than your god, our god's greater than yours / Dagon's greater than Jahweh, Dagon's greater than all . . .*

His body being shaken. "The time is nigh."

He groans and rolls over onto his side.

"Up, man. The army awaits." Lahmi holds forth a cup of strong drink: "Hair of the dog that bit you."

"Go 'way."

Lahmi leans toward him, uses all his strength to hoist Goliath's head up, raises the cup to his lips. "Drink, bro. Drink. The enemy masses upon the opposite hillside. Ye must arise."

"We will win or we will lose . . ."

"We will win."

"Yesterday I scarce dare bid farewell to Asthah. I could not bear the look upon her face."

"What need have you for fond farewells? In yet a few hours the enemy will be routed and you will be home. Sooner than this night shall you see Asthah again; you shall eat the midday meal with her. Within hours will she feed you figs and almonds and rub your skin with fragrant oils."

"Ye speak with such great surety. Yet when a battle is undertaken who but Dagon knows where it shall end?"

"Goliath, none of your philosophy."

From outside the tent Goliath hears the sounds of marching feet as the men form themselves into platoons and then squadrons. Underneath their feet they trample wild sage and rotting figs, releasing smells both sharp and fetid into the air.

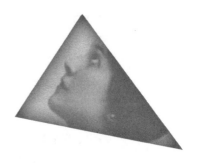

The Blind Marksman

The blindness in this story isn't a metaphor.

Where are you reading this? Maybe you are home on your living-room sofa, pillows propped behind you, feet up on the coffee table, NPR playing in the background. Maybe you're hanging onto a subway strap, taking the D train from Brooklyn into the city. You don't ask, "Why is this sofa here?" "What does this subway strap mean?" The blindness in this story is a solid, meaningless thing, like the sofa or the subway strap.

The blind marksman awakes at dawn in a land far, far away from the land of D trains and radios playing NPR. The country of the blind marksman is rocky and mountainous, and it is only with a tremendous force of will that its people have ever managed to wrest a living from its poor soil. It is also, alas, in between two great land masses that frequently go to war against each other, so that first one side comes tromping across its borders and lays claim to it, and then the other, and then the first side again. This has been going on for millennia.

For the blind marksman dawn isn't rosy-fingered; dawn is the sound of water rumbling and gushing and whistling through the pipes above and below him. His neighbors in the grim block of flats are arising and padding, some in bare feet, some in scuffed brown slippers, to their bathrooms. They are washing themselves; they are emptying their bowels and bladders; some are shaving the hair from their faces. They brush their teeth, ridding their mouths of the aftertaste of the grain liquor they consumed the previous evening. Soon the blind marksman arises; he slips his feet into scuffed brown slippers and pads down the hallway and cleanses himself inside and out; he shaves his face clean.

Next door to this block of flats there is another one, quite identical: the same concrete block construction—indeed, the exact same number of concrete blocks has gone into building it; it, too, sits on a scrub patch of earth; it has people inside it more or less like the ones in the building of the blind marksman; and next to it there is another building, and next to it another one, and so on and so on and so on, all throughout the capital of this beleaguered land.

It would undoubtedly be more pleasant for my reader if I could describe, in addition to these grim buildings built during the Era of Socialist Construction another, older part of the city—perhaps a squat, thousand-year-old Orthodox cathedral across the way from a blue and white mosque; and further tell you that at certain hours the pealing of church bells and the voice of the muezzin calling the faithful to prayer coincide, weaving in and out of each other. But I cannot. In the 1920s this place was chosen as the capital precisely because it had no history, because none of the rival religions and clans and regions of this beleaguered land thought of it as belonging to them. It was merely a place where one changed horses or spent the night on a long journey. It would be something like a truck stop along I-80 in Nebraska being declared our capital. At the center of the town, a number of state buildings grouped around a central square were erected and later these concrete block apartments surrounding them. There are no outskirts to this town: it just ends. And then there are only the winding narrow roads leading into the battered mountains.

The blind marksman goes into the kitchen, where he knows there is no food. Nevertheless he opens the cupboard and there finds only a bag with some flour in it. He can hardly have plain flour for breakfast.

He sits down at the table. One the table is the medal he received for being a blind marksman. The medal is solid in his hand, solid like a sofa or a subway strap or his blindness. He touches it all over; he touches the words engraved on it and he touches the face of the late Great Pilot of Our People, the Beacon of Hope to the Proletarians of the World, the Heroic Leader of the Struggle against the Fascist Invader. He sets the medal back down on the table, sighs, and starts out into the hallway and down the stairs.

This is how the blind marksman became the blind marksman.

When he was seven years old he was sent away from his village in the mountains to a school for blind children; there he learned to read Braille and was one of a small group that sang songs to distinguished visitors about the beauties of his native land and the glories of socialism. He was chosen for this honor because he had a sweet, clear voice and also because he had not, unlike many of his fellow students, been paradoxically blinded by the venereal diseases that had ceased to exist under socialism.

He also learned to mend shoes.

In the Era of Socialist Construction, no longer was the cobbling of shoes to be carried out in small, dusty shops by petty bourgeois entrepreneurs, who might toil on the collective farm by day and then make a few extra *deks* in the evening hammering heels back onto soles and restitching tongues. It was inevitable that such cobblers would find themselves having more than others around them; and having more, they would want more, and thus the whole terrible cycle would begin again. Each nail they drove into a sole would be a nail in the coffin of socialism.

In the glorious new world shoes were to be repaired as part of a state enterprise, and the blind were to be the employees of this enterprise. The blind boy, now a blind youth, went to the capital city and worked in this great undertaking. Every week a truck pulled up and discharged an enormous load of shoes, each pair tied together with a wire that also ran through a yellow tag bearing the name and address of the possessor of the shoes, who was usually going about barefoot while awaiting their return, having no second pair.

(Part of this great enterprise was a vast room where shoes that had become separated from either their opposite number or their yellow tag waited patiently to be reunited with that to which they belonged. Of course, there was also a form (in quintuplicate, please) filled out by those whose shoes did not return from their trip to the city. "Color of shoes?" the form asked, and everyone wrote: "Brown," for no one possessed shoes of any other color; when asked for a description, the befuddled peasants simply wrote the word "Shoes." They could not imagine what else one could say about a pair of shoes.)

The shoes in this land were repaired over and over again; they were soled and resoled; their leather had the texture of the palm of a hand. The humble feet of the proletarians and peasants sweated in these shoes as they labored in their rocky, mountainous fields and trod through barnyards or jumped out of the way of a hot ingot dancing across the floor of a steel mill. Their shoes smelled like old cheese, they smelled like barnyards, they smelled faintly of dead flesh.

During this period, the Era of Socialist Construction, honors were bestowed once a year on the anniversary of the day when the fascists had been driven from the land. It was a known secret that the Great Pilot of Our People, the Beacon of Hope to the Proletarians of the World, the Heroic Leader of the Struggle against the Fascist Invader preferred not to give medals to those who could, in any way, someday pose a threat to him. The Great Pilot of Our People, the Beacon of Hope to the Proletarians of the World, the Heroic Leader of the Struggle against the Fascist Invader preferred to make heroines of women who had given birth to fifteen children and whose bodies were thick and square and spongy and to make heroes of workers who had been terribly maimed in the Battle for Production.

(One year an agricultural worker who had lost a leg rushing to save a child from a threshing machine was nominated for honors by the local branch of the party. His nomination was duly accepted, the required affidavits were obtained, his political and family background investigated, all proved satisfactory and finally, on the great day, he strode across the stage set up in the main square of the capital to receive a medal and a handshake from the Great Pilot of Our People, the Beacon of Hope to the Proletarians of the World, the Heroic Leader of the Struggle against the Fascist Invader. Those whose job it was to read the mercurial moods of the Great Pilot of Our People, etc., understood immediately that a terrible mistake had been made, for the agricultural worker scarcely limped—the loss of the limb had been below the knee. Furthermore, he was square-jawed and rugged and handsome: he looked like a socialist realist painting come to life. Alas, he died in a tragic accident not long after; those who had moved his nomination along were discovered to have engaged in various nefarious schemes for the destruction of socialism and were duly tried, found guilty, and sentenced for their heinous crimes.)

The blind marksman, who was not yet a marksman, believed in the word the way the sighted believe the evidence of their eyes. (Maybe the God of the Gospel According to John was a blind God.) When he heard about the horrors of the war in Viet Nam, they were as real to him as the color brown. He read about the war in Braille and sometimes at night he dreamed the feel of certain words beneath his fingers: *defoliation, Mekong, Ho Chi Minh, massacre.* His friends described for him the picture of a napalmed Vietnamese girl running toward the camera, her clothes and her skin burned off—running from the temple where the people of her village had taken refuge, the temple that had then been bombed by the imperialist aggressor.

You are now to shed that ironical attitude I have worked so hard to awaken in you during the course of this story. You are to think of that feel of napalm on flesh as you think of the marksman's blindness and the sofa and the subway strap.

The Great Pilot of Our People, the Beacon of Hope to the Proletarians of the World, the Heroic Leader of the Struggle against the Fascist Invader said that nothing would stop the imperialist aggressor and that here, too, in this tiny, poor country, they must make ready for the battle that would someday come. The Great Pilot, etc., waxed most eloquent: he said that although their rivers would run red with blood, they would not surrender; the wails of women mourning the dead would resound through all the hills and valleys of this great and poor land, and still they would fight on.

So the blind man learned to be a marksman so he could play a role in the coming battle. It is not as hard to be a blind marksman as many sighted people would imagine. You must stand in exactly the same place on the firing range every time, you must have a furrow against which you always push your toes, and the target must always be placed in the exact same place. You must learn where the butt of your rifle must rest; your bones and muscles must know it to the fraction of a millimeter. Then, once you have got it right, you will hit the bull's-eye every time. (How exactly this skill would be translated to the battlefield is difficult to imagine.)

Soon the prowess of the man on the rifle range came to the attention of the district party leader; the blind marksman was nominated for the highest honor in the land; the man's background was investigated. It was confirmed that not only did he come from the poorest sector of the peasantry but his father and seven of his eight uncles had fought in the War of National Liberation.

On the day of the ceremony a car was sent for him—while he had ridden in buses and trucks, he had never before been in a car—and he was driven to the edge of the great square in the center of the city. There three schoolgirls stepped forward and sang him a song, as he used to sing songs for distinguished visitors to the blind school. His arms were filled with heady-smelling roses. He was led into another car and was driven as part of a motorcade around the streets of the city, past the cheering throngs.

Then the Great Pilot of Our People, the Beacon of Hope to the Proletarians of the World, the Heroic Leader of the Struggle against the Fascist Invader presented the medal to the blind marksman and read out a commendation that stated that the blind marksman could hit moving targets at a range of half a mile and that the blind marksman had trained himself to smell an airplane in the sky long before it could be heard. The blind marksman stood on the stage in front of the cheering throngs with his mouth working like a fish's: he was about to tell the Great Pilot of Our People, etc., that no, it was not true he could hit a moving target at such a range, and as for smelling an airplane in the sky—why, such a notion defied the laws of physics. But how could he possibly publicly contradict such a great man?

The cheering throngs departed. They went home to their apartments made of cement blocks and poured themselves shots of grain liquor. They remembered the original Day of National Liberation. Each of them recalled something from that day with great joy—maybe the quality of exceptionally bright sunlight or the cacophony of all the church bells ringing wildly together or a child standing in the middle of a square, shouting over and over again a word for which she might have been shot for saying the day before.

They could not understand why they were now so unhappy.

Their neighbors came over, each carrying a bottle of grain liquor dangling between two fingers. One neighbor poured the other a drink and said, "The blind marksman can smell an airplane ten miles distant in the sky." He said it with deep devotion.

They drank some more.

After a while one said to the other, "The blind marksman can smell an airplane ten miles distant in the sky," and instead of wiping a tear of socialist pride from his eye he began to laugh. His friend was at first shocked, and then he began to laugh too. They laughed so long and hard that an angry wife appeared in the doorway, her face bruised with sleep, and said, "What's so goddamn funny that you woke me up?" But they were laughing so hard they couldn't say, and she stalked back to bed, muttering, "Everything's an excuse to get goddamn drunk. It's Sunday, no work, he gets drunk to celebrate. Monday, back to work, well, he has to console himself. Day of National Liberation—it's his patriotic duty!"

Within a few weeks, when women had been waiting in line for three hours to buy half a pound of meat, one of them would be sure to say—*If only the blind marksman were here!—The blind marksman?—Yes, don't you know the blind marksman can smell a sheep two hundred miles away, in Italy, even, aim at it, and his bullet will hit so true that it will go straight into the sheep's heart.—But what good does a dead sheep in Italy do us?* And the person who had spoken originally would shrug and say—*Yes, that's why we're waiting in line, in spite of the blind marksman.*

Or when the bus broke down someone was sure to say—*If only the blind marksman were here.—The blind marksman? What would he do?—About a bus that doesn't work? Nothing at all.* And then everyone would laugh.

(This was the sort of humor that flourished under the regime.)

One day the blind marksman was waiting for a bus; the bus stop happened to be next to a public toilet. A woman exited the toilet, releasing an onslaught of foul air as she did so. She took her place in the bus queue, muttering to the woman who happened to be standing next to her about the filth. (She complained only about this single toilet, which was not a crime against the state. If she had said what she wanted to say: *Why is it that our drains are always clogged with filth, that our city has such a rank odor, that we always feel as if we are wading through viscous air when we walk down the street?*—that would have been a crime against the state.) The stranger next to her nodded in weary sympathy and, jutting out her lower lip, said, "If only the blind marksman were here."

The woman nodded and chuckled in response.

"But I am the blind marksman," the blind marksman said.

They began to laugh.

"Why are you laughing?" the blind marksman asked.

"He says *he's* the blind marksman!" the woman called out, and everyone in the line laughed.

A few weeks later the blind marksman was waiting in a line to buy toilet paper, and a woman with tired legs said to another woman with tired legs, "I hear that the blind marksman can shoot rolls of toilet paper out of the sky."

"If only he were here."

"I am here," the blind marksman said, stretching out his hands for the arms of the women. Of course they began to laugh. He tried to explain to them about how the Great Leader had perhaps overstated things a bit, and about the picture of the Vietnamese girl running as her skin was eaten with napalm, and the way he dreamed at night of the feel of the words *Mekong* and *defoliation*, but they only laughed harder.

The blind marksman shouted, "What is so funny?" and then he felt a hand from behind shoving him down to the ground.

(It is my personal opinion that the Great Pilot was like the cooker of kasha who understood that in order to keep the pot from boiling over the lid must be set slightly askew.)

Many years later the imperialist aggressor did come to these shores. He came not in a B52 with canisters of napalm but in a Santa Claus sleigh. He flew over those mountains and villages and muddy, unpaved roads, flinging from his enormous sack bottles of Coca-Cola, televisions, laundry soap, organically grown coffee from the highlands of Guatemala, laptop computers, Mercedes Benzes, sushi, Swatch watches. Santa sent down penicillin, pornography, birth control pills, silk underwear, goose down comforters, and electric wheelchairs. He scattered cameras, costume jewelry, aluminum cooking pans, Georgia O'Keefe prints, video games, cellular telephones, bottles of wine, eyeglasses, cars, sunscreen, seventy-seven different kinds of soap, cashmere sweaters, Johnny Walker Red, jams made from organically grown raspberries, aloe vera lotion, sunglasses, fur coats, down jackets, vermicelli and fusilli wrapped in airtight plastic packages; he shoved out cheap sectional sofas with their joints glued together upholstered in imitation leather, condoms, compact discs of Mozart's Requiem Mass in B Minor and Snoop Doggy Dogg, bagels, polyester clothing in styles that had long since ceased to be fashionable in the West, bottled mineral water, cartons of cigarettes, underwear that came packaged in plastic wrap like the pasta. The bewildered people ran about underneath this rain of gifts. In their eagerness to catch them they jostled each other aside, sometimes even stepping squarely on those who were down in the mud, struggling to get back on their feet. The lucky ones held out their arms to catch the manna from heaven and then staggered under its weight. Others stood resolutely with their arms folded across their chests, saying, "We will not be bought by the capitalists' trinkets," and were then clunked squarely in the head by the outpouring.

"Ho-ho-ho," Santa called as his magic sled flew through the sky. "Ho-ho-ho."

And then one day the state for which the blind marksman had toiled was no more. For a few days afterward the blind marksman reported for work at the shoe cobbling enterprise, but the trucks no longer arrived either to drop off new loads of to-be-mended shoes or to cart just-mended shoes up into the mountain villages along the narrow, winding roads. The People's Printing Office no longer printed either the yellow tags or the quintuplicate forms for the reporting of mislaid shoes.

One by one the other blind cobblers made off with the tools the state had provided for their use: that is to say, they expropriated the means of production. They also took for themselves a goodly share of the shoes that had been cobbled and not yet fetched and those from the vast storeroom waiting to be returned to their long-lost owners. But the blind marksman refused to have any part of this. He showed up every day and sat in the empty room, now silent; that room which had once resounded with the plinking of hammers. It was a crime against the People to do otherwise. His friends, the other cobblers, laughed and said after all, there was no more People, only people, and what was he going to do, sit there forever, waiting for the state to resurrect itself? Why, he might as well wait for the Second Coming of Christ.

But the blind marksman understood that no one had wanted the young girl to run, naked and screaming, from the temple as the napalm burned her flesh—not the photographer whose reputation was made by taking this photograph; not the workers in the napalm factory; not the grocers who sold string beans and chicken to the workers who worked in the napalm factory; not even the simple cobbler in the faraway land who cobbled the shoes of the workers in the napalm factory; not even the man who had flown the airplane—none of them had wanted this to happen, but nonetheless it had happened, and each one—the photographer, the cobbler, the greengrocer, the pilot—was a part of it.

But at last the blind marksman surrendered himself to the reality that there was no path open to him except to become a member of the petty bourgeoisie. So he took the tools he had worked with all these years and went to the square at the center of the capital with a blanket that he spread upon the ground and a sign that said "Shoes Repaired." People came and stood, sometimes like a flamingo on one foot, sometimes their two stockinged feet planted solidly on the cobblestones of the central square, while he repaired their shoes. He handed them their fixed shoes; they handed him the agreed-upon sum of money. The cobbler was moved by the simplicity of this transaction.

Soon the square was transversed by foreigners who had come out of the sky like the capitalists' commodities. Some of them were tourists and some of them were twenty-seven-year-old assistant vice presidents at Chase Manhattan Bank and IBM. The people of this beleaguered land trailed after the foreigners as they walked across the square, or they watched them when they were sitting in a cafe. They were so astonishingly foreign! The shoes of the foreigners were smooth and did not reek of cheese and barnyards and death. One could even imagine that after going about the town for the entire day, carrying their laptop computers and having lunch with this person and coffee with that and handing the person across the table from them a thick gold-nibbed fountain pen with which to sign the papers the foreigners had drawn up, the foreigners would drift back to their hotel rooms together and drink champagne from one another's shoes.

The people were ashamed of having shoes as finely grained with cracks and fissures as the palms of their hands; they were ashamed of having shoes that smelled. They asked the Imperialist Santa for shoes. The next time he flew over their land he showered them with Nikes and Reeboks and black stiletto heels; he flung down Gucci loafers and cheap imitations of Gucci loafers, shoes made of leather and ones made of canvas and plastic. People began to throw their shoes away when the heels wore down or the leather ripped: it was cheaper to buy a new plastic pair. Fewer and fewer people came to get their shoes repaired at the blind marksman's corner of the square.

One day when he was gathering up his things to go home, he discovered a small pile of coins in the corner of his blanket. At first he could not understand what they were doing there. Then the knowledge struck him with the force of a blow: someone had mistaken him for a beggar and set a coin on the corner of his blanket and then someone else, seeing the coin there, had made the same assumption. His first thought was that he would give these coins to one of the beggars who sat near him. But he had so little food in his flat that he slipped the coins into his pocket, feeling like a thief.

Shame was a luxury he could no longer afford.

His sign "Shoes Repaired" came to seem like the signs that are held at busy intersections in the U.S.: "Will Work for Food."

But on this day, the day that began with the dawn sounds of rushings and gurglings in the pipes, when he was sitting on his blanket with his cobbler's tools in front of him and his sign next to him, he heard a series of rapid clicks.

"What is happening?" he called into the air. "What is going on?"

In response he heard only the click-click-click again.

"What are you doing?" he called, with fear in his voice.

A sighted beggar who sat near him called to him, "Don't worry. It's only a foreign photographer. He's taking pictures of you."

"No," the blind marksman shouted to the photographer. "I don't give you permission to take my picture."

The photographer was a young man with a social conscience from a well-to-do family. He might have gone to law school or taken over his father's business, but instead he had become a photographer. He had come here to show the world the devastation that this thing called "freedom" had wrought on this poor land.

"How much do you want?" the photographer said.

"I want nothing from you," the blind marksman shouted.

"It's all right. I'll pay you," the photographer said, shoving several folded bills into the blind marksman's hand.

The blind marksman crumpled up the money and threw it back.

The camera kept clicking.

The blind marksman leaped to his feet. "I repair shoes! I am not a beggar! My name is Memal Keshu. I am the blind marksman. I taught myself to fire a rifle so that I could defend our poor country against the imperialists. I do not give you permission to take my photograph."

Memal Keshu darted about, going after the sound of the camera's click-click-click, but of course the photographer, being much younger than Memal and also sighted, darted swiftly out of his way.

He continued taking pictures.

The first photographs, the ones he had taken before the blind marksman realized he was having his picture taken, showed a face that might have belonged to a Buddhist monk in Viet Nam assuming the lotus position before he set himself on fire to protest the war.

The photographer imagined the caption that might run

under the later shots: "This nation retains its fierce and quixotic pride. A blind beggar becomes angry at a photo-journalist for taking his picture . . ."

Memal Keshu's face burned with rage, and his hands were formed into fists that beat at the empty air in front of him.

The camera kept shooting.

Our Ned

I am not Charlotte Brontë, and this is not a nineteenth-century novel. I know better than to part my hair straight down the middle of my head, a proto–Calvin Coolidge do that makes anyone look altogether too chaste and stalwart. In this text there's no madwoman infected with a dark hereditary taint roistering about in the attic; no heroine yearning for—what exactly is it those Dorotheas and Shirleys and Janes want?—hankering after some—ineffable!—something. No hero out to test his mettle, battered about by the vicissitudes of life, a child of the industrial revolution and bourgeois individualism following the orb of his ambition.

In this story the fools come out of the attic.

And here's Ned Ludd now, clambering down the ladder from the loft above the family's hall, having set a bolt of just-weaved cloth up there, waiting for the clothier, who comes on Tuesday, to fetch it.

Ned Ludd. Hang a little flesh on the bones of those two

words. Not a lot; this was Leicestershire in the waning days
of the eighteenth century and few of Ned's kind were plump.
Although the cottagers hereabouts will soon come to look
back on these days as a time of almost paradisiacal bliss and
plenty, the Ludds ate porridge and milk for breakfast every
morning and too often for supper as well, although sometimes there was bread and rancid bacon and beer for the
nighttime meal, suet dumpling on the odd Sunday.

And from that phrase, "hang a little flesh on his bones,"
the image of a jut of shoulder bone where it joins the clav-
icle: young Ned, a lad of sixteen, shirtless on a hot day in
July, in a cottage where the treadle of a loom worked by
Ned's dad creak-creak-creaked, and the air was filled with
filaments of cotton and linen, white motes dancing in the
shafts of light that streamed through the unshuttered windows. Ned carded the fleece, laying the fibers straight between two steel-pronged brushes; his mam and sister Liza
spun; his brothers George and William were supposed to be
foddering the ox, although they'd taken advantage of their
respite from the watchful parental eye and were having a bit
of a lie-down out in the pasture.

He liked his name, Ned did, the flat-footed spondee of
it, the way his family name echoed his Christian one. Of
course, the curate hadn't said "Ned" when he dabbed his
head with water, for there was no Saint Ned. Edward. A lad's
tongue could get twisted around itself trying to say some
words. The best words were short. Eat. Beer. Gin. Cock.
Cock. That was a good one. Temperance and starvation and
clothier, those were all big words. Ned. Ludd. Simple.

The room smelt of sheep's tallow: so many thousands of
candles had burned in it of a night that the house exhaled a

constant odor of mutton fat. The close air was made closer
still by the fire, on which their evening meal—porridge; you
didn't expect something finer, did you?—was simmering in
a kettle, bubbles of air rising through the thick oats, pucker-
ing the surface and going *phut*.

Ned scratched himself. His ma was a cheery sort, big-
bosomed and quick with a laugh, but not, it must be confessed, the finest of housewives—she'd rather sit by the fire
and warm the soles of her feet than lug the bedding and
straw mattresses out to the yard for an airing and chase the
bedbugs, fleas, and lice with a vinegar-soaked rag, so the
family shared not just collective cottage labour but also a
common itch.

A bead of sweat oozed from a pore above Ned's left nip-
ple, joined with another, and another, and trickled down his
chest. He felt its progress, thought it was a fly crawling along
him, swatted at it, started a little at the dampness, continued
to card the fleece, but his swatting and starting had made his
stroke go off, and one of the spikes gashed open his index
finger. Tears sprang into his eyes.

"Mind!" his father shouted. "You're bleeding all over the
wool."

Ned glared at his dad. Bad temper ran in this family's
blood. His father moved his gaze from his son to the strap
hanging on the wall, gave a "mind yourself" nod to Ned.

"Don't cry, Neddie." His mam bustled about, fetching a
cloth from the cupboard, ripping it into a bandage.

"It hurts."

"Don't coddle the boy. Weak in the head's bad enough."

Further familial pother was prevented by the arrival of
Clever Jack the Methodist, a weaver six days a week and a

preacher on the seventh, a man with a face that could clab-
ber milk. (Perhaps they should have asked Clever Jack to
have a glare at the bedding, and all the mites and midges
therein would be struck stone dead.) But Clever Jack had
his reproving eye on mightier beings than insects—having
just come from dropping his bolts of cloth off at the crop-
pers—and what an occasion for the remonstrance of sin that
was proving to be, what with their gin drinking and general
misdemeaning—and further, he had seen the evidence in
the yard of last night's cock-baiting & dog fighting, and—
and hereat Clever Jack dropt his voice and straightened his
already fearsome backbone, a tall and thin man making
himself even taller and thinner—he suspected whoring, yea!
fornication—at which, Ned's mam glanced over to Ned, but
Clever Jack might have been speaking foreign gibberish for
all it meant to Ned.

Clever Jack continued to expound on divers matters: sin,
sin, and more sin, oppression of the poor in general, the
crimes of landlords—

"Have some beer," said Ned's dad. "Talking's dry work,"
and handed him a mug.

At length, having dispensed with near all the iniquity and
trouble abroad in the land, Clever Jack deigned to ask, "And
how is your family keeping?"

"Well enough. Working hard, the lot of us, but well
enough."

"And how about you, young Neddie?" His voice filled
with false bonhomie.

Ned ducked his head.

"Say 'all right,'" prompted Ned's mam.

"All right," muttered Ned.

"Good lad," Mam said, tousling his hair. "Our Neddie may be thick, but he's got a fine set of teeth." Then, "Go on, open your mouth. Let him see."

"You're right. The Lord's blest you with quite a set of choppers." Clever Jack gave him an amiable cuff on the shoulder, which gave Neddie rather a start.

When at last Clever Jack & Son had departed Ned's dad said, "I reckon he's trying to get us to come to his service of a Sunday. As if we'd want to hear more of his blab."

"He knows a powerful lot of big words," said George.

"Fine words butter no parsnips."

"Are we to have parsnips with butter for dinner?" asked Ned. "Are we?"

A planet, pale blue flecked with white, twirled, as it had for eons, through the blackness of space, rushing along with its sister planets after the sun, like a flock of newly hatched chicks after a brood hen. After eons of long, slow unfurling of life—one-celled organisms becoming two-celled, two-celled becoming four (sing it to a calypso beat: *one-celled, two-celled, three-celled, four*), amoebas evolved and algae, and so on and on and on, until the Earth teemed: lemmings and giraffes and wolves and primates. On a plain on this Earth, a band of simians loped through the long grasses, squatting to eat grubs and ants, finding night shelter beneath the canopy of baobab trees, the trees' blossoms pink cunts that flared open at sunset and gave off a "Hey, sailor" lurid smell, drawing swooping bats that our band of ancestors felled with stones. The mothers and fathers begat sons and daughters, and these daughters and sons begat more sons and daughters, and the first tribe split asunder and asunder again, wandering north and south, east and west. Tectonic plates shifted, continents split, ice slithered down from the polar ice cap and then receded, land bridges rose and fell. They made stone tools and hunted larger prey, woolly mammoths, monkeys, deer—plucked wild plums, ground seeds of grasses between their molars, gave birth to gods and goddesses: Cuchulainn, Yahweh, Kokopelli, Thor, Baba-Yaga. The Age of Stone gave way to the Age of Iron, and no sooner had these sons of man learned how to smelt ore than they figured out how to use iron for weapons—*the better to split your head open, my dear!*; the cities of Uruk and Ur grew up between the Tigris and the Euphrates; the horse was domesticated in the Ukraine; empires rose and fell; gold was traded for salt and later molasses for slaves; peoples hopscotched across the globe—the Aryans flooded into India; the Mongols pushed the Turkic peoples west; the Bantu pulsed out from central Africa; the Goths, the Visigoths, the Ostrogoths, the Vandals sacked Rome. Now back to that planet, hurtling itself through space. Europe descended into the long torpor of the Middle Ages. Then ships began to travel forth from Lisbon, from Genoa, from Southampton, spreading the world open to the European colonists; the Enlightenment shone the harsh light of rationality into every heretofore shadowy nook. The long sleep of unreason was beginning.

Ned liked to go down Sheepwash Lane and over the stone bridge across Rothley Brook and into the woods. In a glade made by the sheltering branches of an ancient oak, he twirled himself dizzy, the branches and the sky and the mottled loam of the earth reeling themselves around him. A sweet kind of a fuddle it was, not like when his dad thwacked him.

As he lay on the ground he heard a fragment of a song, half sung, half whispered: *If ponies rode men and if grass ate the cows* . . . The tune was being sung by Richard Sloper, a man who wouldn't be out of place in a nineteenth-century novel. Richard's father was a successful clothier—that is, he led a line of pack mules that weekly carried raw bales of cotton, wool, and flax to the cottagers and picked up the finished cloth they had woven, took it to market, saw that it fetched a fair price—or, if it fetched an unfair price, that the inequity inured to the elder Sloper's advantage—purchased more raw materials, loaded them onto his pack mules, and began again on his rounds. He was a man most indulgent toward his only son; it was his deepest wish that Richard might spend his life pursuing his scientific interests as one of better birth would be able to, unhampered by the crass concerns of money-getting.

For Richard, there was no greater pleasure than walking in the woods, but he did not dally thereabouts. He was diligent—always with his notebook and charcoal tucked in his satchel, his head bent down, searching for an as yet unnamed plant, seeking to lay the grid of Linnaean botanical classification over the wild profusion of nature, to sketch exactly the arrangement of the stamens and the shape of the petals of his specimens; to save a plant by pressing it and adding it to his private museum. Richard had already had several letters published in the *Proceedings of the Royal Botanical Society*, and hoped he might have the chance to venture beyond the environs in which he had been raised to pursue his searches on the arid plains of the Hindu Kush or in the lush jungles of Borneo.

And cats should be chased into holes by the mouse . . .

Liza had said if you caught a fairy you could pull its wings off and keep it in your pocket and make it do your bidding.

"You're a man," Ned said.

"What did you think?"

"I dunno." He knew were he to say sprite or fairy the man would laugh. "You'll get your britches dirty."

"You're one to talk," the stranger said fondly.

"But you've got fancy ones."

The man was hunkered down by a plant, drawing a rough sketch of it with a charcoal pencil.

"You draw real good. You can write, too. I can't write, but I know writing when I see it. What's that word?"

"*Aethusa.*"

"And that one?"

"*Cynapium.*"

"Is that your name?"

"No, it's the name of the plant."

"Not that one there. That one there is fool's parsley."

"That's its common name. *Aethusa cynapium* is its scientific name."

"It give off a powerful nasty pong. When you pick it. I brought it home to my mam, I thought it was parsley, and she said, get that stinking stuff out of my house. Out of my house."

The man rubbed a leaf between his thumb and index finger, lifted it to his nose. "Right you are. Perhaps one day we shall have a way of quantifying smells. But for now I shall just note, "Bruised leaves emit foul odor.""

The lad was restless, couldn't stop moving. He had an odd, bumble-footed gait that gave him the appearance of forever being about to trip over his toes and fall forward, and then, just before he stumbled, recovering himself, only to take another step in a similar manner.

"Say that I'm the one what telled you that. Write my name in your book. Ned. Ned Ludd is my name."

"One 'd' or two?"

"Huh?"

"Never mind."

"You're clever, aren't you? I am foolish, my mam says, but not entirely a fool. Only on account of Liza dropping me on the head when I was a babe . . . Am I vexing you? I do that sometimes. I vex folks. I ask too many questions. Am I asking too many questions?"

"It's all right," said Richard, setting down his sketchbook.

"I know someone else clever," Ned said. "Clever Jack the Methodist. He's powerful clever, is Clever Jack."

"Well, he certainly seems to be well named." Richard took his farewell. He knew he would get precious little else accomplished with this village simpleton traipsing after him.

Wandering home, Ned saw a wash of red amidst the mottled brown and green. The dead body of an animal, he knew it. He gave the corpse a poke with a stick, watched a cloud of black flies rise up. He flipped it over and saw it was a hedgehog. Worms and maggots had already eaten away its eyes.

He ran, legs and arms windmilling, chest aching, home to his mother, ran as if he could outrun his sick terror of death—of the rot and stink of it—crying, "Mam, Mam, I don't want to die! I don't want to die!"

"You won't die, Neddie. You won't die." His mother held him, pressing his head against the two overstuffed pillows of her breasts.

"All that is flesh passeth away," said his dad.

"Will I rot in the ground?"

"You'll leave your body behind like a husk, and your soul will fly to heaven to be with Jesus, and then on the day of judgment, your soul and your body will be reunited," his mother assured him. Not much for religion, these Ludds, but then again, not above using it when it suited them.

His mother's words offered him no comfort; in fact troubled him more: the thought of his soul watching his rotting corpse for long millennia while vermin and insects gnawed at his flesh.

"I don't want it to happen. I'm scared."

"Oh, for the love of Jesus, have some gin and quit your moaning."

"Yes, lad." For once Ned's mother agreed with his dad. "A drop of strong water will ease your pain."

So Ned had a drop, Ned's mam had a drop, George had one, as did Liza, as did William, as did Ned's dad—it was just the thing for his lumbago—and then, that made them feel so good, they had another and then another.

"All right," said Dad, "enough larking about. Now back to work."

"A toast to hard labour. May he rest in peace." Mam knocked her mug against those of George and William and Ned and tried to click it against Liza's, but she said, "Dad's right. The clothier will be here on Tuesday."

"Tuesday?" said Mam. "Oh, Tuesday's a long way off."

"Let's raise a glass to Tuesday."

"Tuesday!"

"Tuesday!"

"Tuesday!"

"May it stay well away."

"Now see here, woman—"

"Huzzah for Tuesday!"

"I'll not be mocked," shouted Dad. "Not under my roof."

"Whose roof? It was my grandfather what built this cottage."

"Wives, submit to your husbands," yelled Dad, going for the strap.

"You leave my mam alone!"

Ned's mother was on her feet now, her hands on her boy's shoulders: "Neddie. Keep your temper in check, lad. It'll be all right."

"Neddie," Dad mocked, his voice falsetto. "Keep your temper in check. It'll be all right."

"Take Ned out the cottage," Mam ordered George and John.

"Come on, Ned."

"No. Mam! Mam! I won't let him take the strap to you!"

"This is what comes of drinking gin in the afternoon," screamed Liza.

And Ned broke free of his brothers' grasp, grabbed the poker from the hearth, swung it above his head. His heart galloped; his breath came ragged and fierce. Usually his mam smelled like yeast and his dad like old leather, but now he could smell the acrid scent of fear pulsing from their bodies. He could bring this poker down on his dad's head, crack open his skull, and his brains would come slithering out. Death was inside all of us, waiting, waiting.

"Don't raise your hand against your father! Ned, promise me just one thing: that you won't hit your father!"

"No one better come near me," Ned cried, holding the poker above his shoulder.

"Ned. It's your mam who has never ask't anything before of you. Promise me you won't touch your dad. Neddie, promise?"

"I promise," Ned said, but he kept swinging the poker, back and forth, back and forth. It was glorious to behold the darting eyes of his dad in fear, like a trapp'd animal.

"Neddie. Neddie. You promised."

"I promised," Ned shouted, as he brought the poker down on the wooden strut of the loom. What a sound, that crack of wood! And the collective in-gasp of breath by the family. And again. "I promised. I promised I wouldn't—"

"Neddie, not the loom."

"—not take the poker to Dad," and brought it down harder yet against the wood. "But I didn't say nothing about the loom."

"Neddie, Neddie, darling! Stop! Stop!"

But he didn't stop, not until it lay on the floor all smashed to bits, utterly and completely undone.

Dad and Liza and the brothers tried to set the loom to rights, fitting the shattered pieces back together, boiling cattle hooves to make glue, wrapping the broken bits with warp-string, but try as they might, they couldn't get it set to rights. The clothier—Richard Sloper's father, as it happened—was the owner of the loom, and was not inclined to put another in the home where that idiot might have at it again. Ned's mum slept next to him that night and for nearly a week after, so afraid she was that Ned's dad or his brothers might do him in at night.

"A fiend, a very devil," his dad could be heard muttering over his gin as he sipped it beyond the front door. "Our ruin. The lad should have been drowned in the river—"

146

"You shut your drunken mouth," Mam shouted out the door. "You lay a hand on my son and I'll see you hanging from the gibbet!"

Folks took to saying, when the workings of a loom got bollixed up, "Looks like Ned Ludd's been here," or, when out of temper with their employer, "I've a mind to Ned Ludd it."

And Richard Sloper, the gentleman with the notebook Ned met near Rothley Brook? About two weeks after his encounter with Ned, he returned home to find his father feverish—a nicked finger had gone septic—and within a week the illness ended in his untimely death, forcing young Sloper to abandon the pursuit of his scientific interests and enter into the hurly-burly of the mercantile realm. His father's demise also revealed that the elder gentleman—who had seemed to all the world quite prosperous and staid—was in fact deeply in debt, and his son was forced to scramble not only to provide the barest sustenance for his mother and sisters but also to keep the world from uncovering the chaotic state of his father's affairs, as his creditors, who had been kept at bay by his father's expansiveness and air of good fortune, now descended like a flock of kites on a just-cold corpse.

Young Sloper sometimes felt as if he, too, had entered the grave. His very aspect was so changed—his posture stooped, his brow furrowed—that more than once an acquaintance of his youth passed him on the street and thought: That man looks familiar. Why yes, he reminds me of Richard Sloper; perhaps that's some relation—an elder brother or uncle. As in his appearance, so in his character: resignation to the harshness of life, the gradual extinction of dreams and fantasies that usually happens slowly in a man's character through the years from youth to middle age occurred almost overnight in him.

About a year after his father's passing, Sloper—he thought of himself by his surname now—went into his study on a Sunday afternoon and took his illustrated notebooks down from the shelf and undid the ties on them but found he could not bear to look at them, to recall the delight he had taken in mixing his inks to capture exactly the hue of nature, his dreams of traveling to some land where no civilized man had yet been. He threw his drawings into the fire along with his pressed plant specimens. His once-precious volumes of Voltaire, Rousseau, Locke, and Newton grew dusty on the shelves.

But he did not entirely abandon his interest in scientific pursuits. After nearly ten years, through great frugality and even greater industry, his father's debts were at last discharged. Through all those bleak years, Sloper held one hope—the idea had come to him slowly, accreting itself layer by layer as the pearl is formed within a patient mollusk—that he might apply scientific principles to the affairs of business. He led his pack mules round about the cottagers, dropping off the raw materials and picking up the finished, because this was what his father had done before him. What changes there were in the methods of manufacturing seemed to come about haphazardly. Suppose rather than following custom he took stock of the situation, rationalized his business dealings, thought of them as a series of great experiments? Would it not be more efficient to gather workers together in a manufactory, with the power of steam-driven machines to do what the power of the human body now did? And since the operation of these looms would require but little strength, the work could be done, not by the current weavers whose demand for wages made the cloth dear, but by women and even children. In the factory, eliminated also would be variations in the cloth—not only was that of Thomas Brigham always woven too tightly and that of Lester Ballford too loose, but Sloper could trace the patterns of a weaver's day as he examined the textile: the texture fine and regular at the start of the morning, then errors creeping in as the day wore on and the weaver's attention flagged. He would be a god over this minor kingdom, setting down the order of things. Was it blasphemy to think such a thought? No—surely it was not sacrilege to use reason—the greatest of God's gifts—to throw off the sad old bonds of superstition—to shape the world over which man had been given dominion. He knew there would be opposition; threats and perhaps even violence from those whose old and established ways were being overturned—had not the inventor of the spinning jenny, himself a once-poor weaver, found himself attacked by his former fellows, driven from his Blackburn home?—but Sloper determined to do what was right, as against what was easy.

He began to sketch—not with the carefully colored inks he had once used to draw his botanical observations but in quick India black—the plan for a great factory. He would not borrow, he would not encumber—no, he would not allow himself to be trammeled by what had ensnared his father. The substantial portion of his earnings that had once gone to the discharge of the old debts was now stockpiled; his mother and sisters lived as they had been accustomed to living—although the house they had inherited was grander than those of the weavers, neither their victuals nor their raiments was any finer.

Ned's mam and dad soon went to their Rest, few made old bones in those days. The cottage got sold to keep the family from starving; consumption got George; Liza married a man from another shire; John hied himself off to America, the leech that bleeds the excess population from these lands, perhaps becoming the ancestor of the North American branch of the family, an Alfred and an Ada Ludd, a Waldo and a Fanny who will pop up in early twentieth-century census records in Denver and Altoona, Pa; William went to the fair in Loughborough and never returned—whether he was set upon by scoundrels, impressed into the Navy, balloted as a soldier, or what, none knew; and our Ned was left alone.

Ned walked. He walked because he was walking. He walked because he was hungry, and the walking distracted him from the pangs in his belly. He walked because he did not know what else to do.

Along a lane he encountered an old woman who gave him a cup of buttermilk but told him not to lollygag around there: her husband had got a frightful temper. He slept in the hollow of a half-burnt tree and woke up with bugs and spiders and worms crawling all over him, which gave him a fright he'd woken up dead. He knew the first thing they eat is your eyes, because your eyeballs are made of treacle and jelly. He tried to touch them to see if they were still there, but his lids kept closing over them.

A dog chased him and he ran. He found a dead squirrel by the side of the road, built a fire, and ate it. He came in to a town; he asked someone where he was. "Paris, France." Later he learnt the truth: Leicester. He passed a man with stumps for legs wearing a sign about his neck.

"What's that say? The writing?"

"Born crippled."

"Where did your legs go?"

"A devil took them. While I was in my mother's womb."

"My sister drop't me on the hearth. That's why I'm foolish. I'm hungry," Ned said.

The crippled man took him up an alley, pulled a goodly hunk of cheese from his pocket, broke it in two pieces, giving Ned the larger.

"I filched it. From the shop over by the church. Teach him a lesson. Folk should mind their goods better."

"Good cheese," Ned managed around a mouthful. Then: "What's he want with them?"

"Who?"

"The devil what took your legs."

"The ways of the demons are legion and mysterious."

Caleb and Ned slept together that night, sharing the warmth from one another's bodies.

"He give that to you?" Ned asked the next day. "Instead?"

"Who?"

"The devil what took your legs."

"No. Old Crankton. Well, hired it out to me. It's called a tambourine."

"Big word," Ned said.

They traded Ned's shoes for a cloth cap and by the Corn Exchange Caleb danced on his odd stumps of legs and Ned passed the hat.

Tut, tut, the ladies said, passing by. *Oh, dear me, I can't look*, but they did nothing but look. Caleb hollered after one skinflint: "You stopped and had a good gawp, mate. Pay up!"

Thursday was market day, and Caleb reckoned they'd do well, but folks were distracted by a learned pig a local farmer was showing off for a farthing.

A pair of spectacles was a fine thing for allowing to slip down the bridge of one's nose and then staring over, as one of the bank of overseers of the parish poor did, asking a series of questions:

"Your name?"

"Ned, sir."

"Surely Edward."

"Edward, sir."

"And?"

"And, sir?"

"And your surname, man?"

"Lud, sir. My name was longer—Ludlum, I think, or Ludham, something like that—but my tongue would always get confused, so my mam said we'll make it Lud. Ned Lud. "

"Now, your mother gave birth to how many children?"

"I don't know."

"You don't know?" A bit of phlegm in the throat was almost as good as a pair of spectacles, for the noise that can be made when the throat was cleared, a sound that suggested simultaneously disapproval and disgust.

"Had she ten? Twenty? Thirty?"

"Not thirty, sir. Thirty's a powerful lot."

"Well. Do you know how many survived infancy?"

"There was me. George. Mary. The two Williams."

"Two Williams?"

"When one died, she named the next William, too. Sir. An elder and a younger."

"Rather like the Pitts," the overseer said, glancing first to his left and then to his right at the other overseers, who each returned his look with a facial expression closer to a sneer than a smile.

"John. Me. Of course me. Liza."

"Liza? Liza? Surely she was not christened Liza."

"Elizabeth, I imagine it was," said one of the others, shifting a bit in his chair to show his discomfort: certainly those who came before the parish in need of sustenance must be questioned, but it was clear that this man before them was half-witted at best.

The fates of all the family members were gone over: dead, dead, went to the fair and never come back, gone to America, destitute himself.

"And what about other relations? Have you no friends?"

"There's many folks as are fond of me. But none I know has aught to spare."

"Now, you do understand, don't you, that begging is a criminal offense?"

Ned wasn't sure if he was supposed to answer that question yes or no, so he hung his head and both nodded it slightly and shook it slightly while muttering "Sir."

"And those companions you fell in with in Leicester. They are a bad sort, and you are to steer clear of them, and others like them."

"No, sir."

"No?"

One of the other men leaned forward and said, "I believe

the man is confused." Then to Ned: "You want to be good, don't you?"

"Yes, sir. I want to be good, sir. I want to go to heaven and be with my mam."

Ned was farmed out by the overseers to work in the house of a weaver along with a gang of others, mostly old women and children. He was fed gruel and skilly and milk pottage, beer and cheese for Sunday dinner, and carded rough cotton, day in, day out; the hours of work stretched from first light to last, and so he loved the winter, despite the cold, for the shortness of the days. Sometimes he sneaked off with Old Maude and she sucked his nob behind the jakes, and he was in such heaven he hardly noticed the privy stink.

Sloper felt the winds of history breathing down his neck. The notion of a manufactory, of mechanisation, that had grown up in his mind had also grown in the minds of a dozen—nay, a hundred—other men, so that it almost seemed the notion had spread via contagion. He knew he must get a foothold in this new enterprise or he would be shut out from it altogether. Flocks of geese flew west from the linen fields of Flanders crying out, "Expand! Expand! Or die! Or die!" their honking growing deeper as they traveled into the distance, spreading the alarm: "Expand! Or die!" Sloper broke the vow he had made never to encumber himself with debt, borrowing in order to purchase a parcel of land.

The copse in which his factory was to be erected was quickly cleared, gangs of itinerant farmhands and Irish labourers tearing from the ground the confusion of brambles and grasses as they plunged their shovels into the yielding earth. The sleeping larks, disturbed before full light by the commotion, launched themselves heavenwards, not in exultation but with a full-throated cry of alarm. The eagles and the martens, the polecats, the ravens, the weasels, the voles that had once made this glade their home fled, none knew where. Soon the bricks were laid, one atop the other and the other and the other. The building rose six stories high: twenty-four windows on the side facing east and twenty-four windows on the west-facing side; twelve each on the sides facing north and south. Atop it all a great chimney, which soon belched a black cloud of coal smoke into the air; from below the works evacuated its dejecta into a nearby river, making it a cesspool. One might have assumed that Sloper, who had once been so enamored of the natural world, might have felt a pang of guilt at so despoiling it, but he had instead a sense of gleeful retribution, as if Nature had abandoned him, and he were now visiting his vengeance on her.

Sloper did not sleep easy; in fact, he slept only to wake with a racing heart and a sense of panic: his debt, his very being pledged to others, the thing he had most valued, his independence—in jeopardy; mostly he was haunted by the two letters received in the past week, one written in a hand most fine: *The Machines have thrown thousands of your petitioners out of employ, whereby they are brought into great distress, for we are made slaves to things inanimate, and shall come to envy the Africans who labour in the sugar fields of the West Indies, who at least are provided with sustenance by their owners, while to us a grain of wheat has come to seem as precious as a ruby or an emerald. We honest workingmen are being improved to death. Shall not the justice of man as well as the judgment of the Almighty shall be visited on those who make their riches on the ruin of their fellow men?* The other writ in a crude hand:

If you bring dev'l machines here you will be deserving of the gibbet and that is what you shall get, both signed N. Ludd, the first with the honorific "Captain" preceding it, the second with the bare name followed by the address: *His office, Sherwood Forest.* The week before he'd received reports of machine-manufactured cloth being set afire in Leeds; and just last week Josiah Slocum's man, escorting machinery along a lane by night, had been set upon and killed, and it was clear it was no ordinary highway robbery, for his purse had been left untouched. It was blasphemy to do so but Sloper thought of God beset by Satan's rebellion in the midst of his plan of Creation.

From a distance of half a mile the sound given off by the factory seemed to be a hum, not unlike that made by a swarm of bees returning to its hive with the product of its labour; but as one drew closer the rumble not only grew louder but became a series of distinct sounds: the steady clang of cast iron against cast iron, the queer skirls of a thousand spinning bobbins and spindles. Indeed, the human voice could not make itself heard amidst the terrible din, and the labourers soon developed a system of signs and meemaws, whilst the foremen spoke the language of the strap. Sloper could not enter his own premises without in short order developing a pounding headache, and wondered how his hands could bear it all the day.

One day during his weekly perambulation across the factory floor he glimpsed a strange figure and he suddenly felt as if a cold hand had gripped his heart. Was he on the verge of a stroke, apoplexy? It rushed back to him—the last time he had walked in the woods before his father's death—the dullard he'd encountered there, the curious lad with the queer manner of walking. The sharp edge of sorrow changed to a knife blade of disgust. In nature one such as he—the runt of the litter—would have been shunted aside, left to perish, the weak giving way before the strong. He motioned to his foreman, and the two walked into the relative quiet of the yard.

The foreman answered Sloper's questions: the man was a half-wit, let out to the factory by the man charged with his care by the parish overseers.

"This is most irregular. I am not running a charity."

The foreman objected: the man was no object of charity. If he had a fault it was a tendency towards being too persevering—set to a task, he would keep at it, at it, at it.

"Is he some relative of yours?"

The foreman denied this but allowed as how their two fathers had known one another.

Sloper had no need of giving a direct order; the look of disapproval on his face said all that needed to be said, and Ned was dismissed.

This pale blue planet continues to hurtle itself through space, while that tribe of ex-simians continues on its journey into the light. In revolutionary France, everything was made rational, even time itself—the calendar beginning over at Year Zero, the old units of measure—based on the amount of land two oxen could plow in a day or the distance along the outstretched arms of a man—replaced by the meter, the centimeter, the millimeter. The words of the philosophers were shouted upon the barricades. The very Earth found her skin rent by the makers of bricks, who quarried the ancient clay beds, taking that old stuff—odd bits of metal left from the Big Bang, the shells of mollusks, plankton, and krill that died eons upon eons before Ned Ludd's ancestors walked the Serengeti—and firing it into bricks, bricks, and more bricks, bricks to make factories, bricks to make row houses to house the workers for said factories, bricks to make asylums for the weak and feeble. Bricks bricks bricks bricks bricks bricks bricks. The guillotine and the Terror followed the bliss of Revolution—become a sow that eats her farrow—and now Napoleon spread liberty across Europe by the sword—which had led to England's Orders in Council embargoing trade with any nation that trafficked with France, thereby cutting off the Americas and wrecking Midland weavers, who furthermore were undercut by the new manufactories. Bolts of cloth were piling up in lofts and storerooms, bolts of fustian, bolts of linsey-woolsey, bolts of twill, bolts of burlap, bolts of dimity, bolts of muslin.

Which brings us now to anno Domini 1811. A lurid comet has been crashing across the heavens like a sword aflame, perhaps seeding pestilence and discord, and Nature herself seems in rebellion: in June it had been so cold ice appeared in the River Irk and now we find ourselves in a hot October. Babes die at the dry teats of their famished mothers.

The only sound the crowd of men made moving through the night was the basso profundo of their tromping footsteps, with an occasional slurp as a boot unstuck itself from muck and mire. Still it was enough of a sound to startle the flocks of tits roosting in the bushes, which flung themselves upward with an alarmed chatter and rush of wings as Ned Lud's army marched past them. The faces of the men were blackened with charcoal, others hidden—all but the eyes—with kerchiefs folded into triangles, like outlaws in old-time Westerns, yet others dressed in women's clothes, frocks and bonnets above hobnail boots. Those men who were by natural formation gaunt have been rendered by the force of the famine now abroad in the land positively cadaverous.

Light, faint but constant, shone from a crescent moon, the mob of stars above. The torches the plodding men carried brought certain things into high contrast—now the gnarled roots of trees, now the shining eyes of badgers, polecats, foxes disturbed on their nocturnal rambles, cowering in the gorse.

At the front of the parade was Ned Lud, that is the scaffolding of his name, with the addition of the honorific "General"—Leader of the Army of the Distressed and Wrecked Weavers and a Friend to the Poore!—and a pair of patched and mended breeches stuffed with straw, a swallow-tailed jacket of navy-colored fustian. A bit of gold gimcrack tacked onto the shoulders and cuffs was meant to impart an overall military sense, as was the cap set atop his muslin-and-batting head, although the men who have made him have certainly never seen a general, never mind the cap of one. A pole up his backside, for he was borne aloft, arms and legs flopping this way and that.

At the gate of the mill the throng paused. A few men had pots of ale, and who wouldn't like a gulp of courage at a moment such as this? Men slugged it back, passing the jars from one to another, formed their hands into rough cups and slurped from them. One whispered to the man next to him, "At least I'll die with the taste of ale in my mouth." The one whispered to thought, "Die. Die," and his knees started to wobble.

And then the crowd made a noise which could perhaps be described as a holler or a yowl; at any rate, it is a word that cannot be written save with a string of caroming vowels. Perhaps it is the bellow the Luddites' stomachs, cramped with starvation, would have given off had the individual organs within them the power of direct speech.

The language ceased to be Pentecostal; it shattered itself into individual words:

"Hurrah! Ned Ludd!"

"Down with all kings but King Lud!"

"Now to the gates!"

Which were in short order broken down, and then the rioters had at the machines with blacksmiths' hammers, the butt ends of farm implements, muskets, blunderbusses. Smithereens! Time ran backward. All those long, long hours spent making those machines were undone; the black ore, mined out of Satan's bowels, the tempering, the casting, the fitting together into those mechanical looms, all turned to naught.

A fire was kindled; a voice called, "All out!" and Ned was flung through the air, landing atop the fire, the flames flaring through his straw limbs and belly, for none dared march off with him, as he had become evidence which could indict a man for the capital offense of machine wrecking, so his immolation became General Ludd's last act, at least in this scene of the drama.

The *Oxford English Dictionary* cites Pellew's *Life of Lord Sidmouth* (1847) as the source for the story about the youth of weak intellect who smashed the looms in a Leicestershire village, although there is an earlier version of it in *The Beggar's*

Complaint, Against Rack-Rent Landlords, Corn Factors, Great Farmers, Monopolizes, Paper Money Makers, and War, and many other Oppressors and Oppressions, Also, Some Observations on the Conduct of the Luddites, In Reference to the Destruction of Machinery, &c., &c., authored by "One who Pities the Oppressed" in 1813. But perhaps the locals were pulling the leg of Lord Sidmouth, who'd been sent to lead the army that put down the Luddite rebellion. One alternative etymology posits that "Lud" is derived from the Latin word for play, *ludus*. The Luddites—dressed in women's clothes or with coal-blackened faces—were marching underneath a figure representing merrymaking and fun, out to destroy the grim factories. The Norse word *ludden* (thick), from which is derived a synonym of buttocks, luds, offers yet another possibility: the Luddites celebrating their rear ends, their holy backsides—our sweet arses, which reason and logic can go kiss.

So perhaps there never was a Ned; perhaps Liza never did drop him on his head on the bricks by the hearth; perhaps he never did clamber over the stone hedge and wander in the woods; perhaps he never did get examined by the poor-law administrators; perhaps he never did sit, slack-jawed and missing his mam, carding cotton and looking for a chance to sneak off with old Maude—thick Ned, dull Ned, our Ned.

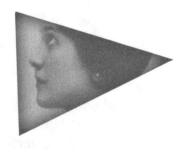

Moby Dick, or, The Leg

Bloomings

Call me Ahab.

What's in a name? A rose by any other name would smell as sweet, as the Bard once said. Although, alas, he couldn't have foreseen today's hybridized, gene-monkeyed floral races, bred to bloom in uniform, boring splendor on the 14th of February or some other day—Secretaries' Day! Grandparents' Day! Bosses' Day! Aye, Bosses' Day!—which the florists have decreed must stir a sentiment within our hearts which cannot be expressed save by the purchase of a dozen or two of these overbred perfect monstrosities, still called roses but smelling nowhere near as sweet. A pox on Luther Burbank and all his tinkering progeny! But I digress—or do I?

Do not think me ignorant of that other tome, penned by a lowly seaman under my command who dubbed himself Ishmael. (Although he neglected to mention that aboard the

Pequod he—a ginger-haired lad with a bouncing, prominent Adam's apple and goggle eyes—was known by the diminutive "Ish.") Ah, Ishmael! You of the pierced nose and dirty T-shirt, lounging in the dark corner of a grungy coffeehouse, nursing a bitter single espresso and a depression!

In Ish's account he had no surname and I had no Christian one—as if mine own dear wife might murmur in my ear on an intimate occasion, "Captain! Yes, Captain! Stave on! I am almost in port, Captain!" Ishmael, son of a dark woman of the desert, no patronymic, wanderer, owing fealty and bond to no man; and Captain Ahab, a man known by his title and his clan, tied to wife and babe, beholden to those who have sent him out on this voyage, a man of substance, even if some of that substance be whalebone.

It was said that my name should not fill one with pride: for when the biblical Ahab died the dogs did lick his blood. Who do ye think shall feast on that hunk of animated meat you are when the spirit passes from it? If in a graveyard ye are interred, maggots and worms shall slither over thee—ye shall be digested by a most lowly order. A watery bower thy last sleeping place? Full fathom five, don't hope for bones turned into coral or pearls for eyes—it's a slimy business down there, too. Choose fire and ye are but pollution for the air. I can think of few finer ends for any body than to be recycled in canine flesh. Lap on, curs!

Where was I? Ah, yes. What's in a name? A rose, etc. Ms. Stein adds: Rose is a rose is a rose. Much discussion could go into that sentence, which we have not the time for here—for it seems we are allotted but the space of a short story. Ish was given a whole book; he was permitted the space to ramble through the subject of fast-fish and loose-fish, to contemplate the philosophic import of the sperm whale's lacking a nose, to speak of the possible routes the whale that bore Jonah might have taken—while I, I am truncated, reduced, cut short. Such is my fate. I must hold the elbows of my narrative tight against my literary sides; I must squeeze myself into the shortened shift of this abbreviated form. Why? Because the modern reader has not the time; she won't sit still for long disquisitions. A century and a half ago having one's morning toast involved the baking of the bread, and not some concoction quickly whipped up in a bread machine—no, the flour must have been sifted, the yeast proofed in slightly heated water, the dough kneaded and set out to rise, the wood-fired oven tended while it baked—whereas now you think yourself industrious, a veritable homebody, if you make yourself a slice of toast instead of dashing into Bruegger's Bagels (by the way, I know you parked illegally in handicapped parking when you did so—and don't you go whimpering, "But all the other spaces were full! I was only two seconds!") and grabbing a cinnamon raisin. To wash your clothes you have no need of scrub boards, no soaps you yourself have concocted with treasured fat culled from pig and goat and sheep and cooked with lye. No, you merely dump in the dirty garments, pour some liquid from a plastic jug, push a button—but with all that, you are so busy saving time you can't spare enough to plough your way through an entire novel; you swallow a short story as you down your daily tablets of vitamin C and gingko extract. The more time you save, the less you have. Weren't you told what you seek to keep you lose? But did you listen? No, you never do.

Well, we haven't gotten off to a very good start, have we?

You've no doubt written me off as a cantankerous old cripple by now, lurching about on my whalebone leg and scattering aspersions where I will. Well, this is a work of art, not a popularity contest. Ye need not love your narrator: ye need only hear him out.

Hear. Yes, that reminds me. Back to good Gertrude: the spoken version of her most famous epigraph sounds rather like: Eros is eros is eros. Amongst the other possible readings you might decipher from that plainest of palimpsest is this: the word writ by the finger on the page is one thing, the word as it hums and hisses its vibrato upon the tympanic membrane of the ear quite another.

And so your narrator would be most appreciative if you, good reader, as well as perceiving this text through your eyes, could imagine it being read aloud—and, moreover, read by someone with a rolling, profound, stentorian voice. Hear Jahweh herself—or, better yet, Barbara Jordan—intoning the words here writ.

Now, fair reader, if I may be permitted to guess at the thoughts that are currently in your mind: How comes this man Ahab to know of Barbara Jordan, Gertrude Stein, Bruegger's Bagels, and the text by young Ish writ? For he was drowned, was he not, and the sole survivor of that literary disaster being Ishmael, AND-I-ONLY-AM-ESCAPED-ALONE-TO-TELL-THEE Ishmael? Was it not so?

No, it was not.

I was on a later voyage shipwrecked; but on the one where Ish was under my command we returned to Nantucket, our holds stuffed full with oil and near my whole crew intact. (Half a decade later my craft was dashed on some South Sea shoals and I eventually washed up on the shore of an isle, yet still uncharted, where the inhabitants possess a marvelous fruit which prolongs longevity beyond all previous limits: and so I survived, while the decades turned into a century and then beyond—still one-legged, of course, at times a bit soft in the head—although, on this atoll, where great age is held a blessing, a high compliment is paid when it is said, "His mind has begun to wander," for they think this to be the richest kind of thought. At any rate, this is how I come now to be tapping out this story on the keys of a computer.)

So, having got that bit of narrative tomfoolery out of the way, let us swim back to the beginning of our text.

My name begins with no phallic "I" but a letter "A," two legs spread open, a hole to receive. When type was hand-set the letter "A" could be picked up, held in the hand: it had a weight. Type with a cracked leg or missing serif was called crippled type. My "A" is a crippled letter, with one leg cracked, dismasted, dead-stumped. Such crippled type was thrown into a special box, to be melted down and made anew. But I refuse to be smelted. I aim to write this text with crippled type. But . . . where was I? Oh, yes, right back at the beginning; I hadn't even weighed anchor, so to speak.

Plunging On

Well, it seems I am not to be given the space to wander at liberty about New Bedford, to inform my reader of how I slept and with whom, of where and upon what I breakfasted and dined; no, it is not given to me to deck out my tale as the *Pequod* was bedecked: no polished gimcracks shall ornament this opus, I shall hang no trophies upon her frame, no verbal sea-ivory shall her embellish. No etymology of

the words "crip," "freak," "amputee" supplied by a late con-
sumptive usher to a grammar school shall front this text, nor
extracts from great texts on our condition set down by the
pen of a sub-sub-librarian.

A mere thousand-something words down and I am
plunged upon the waters of the cold Atlantic. Let us put it
briefly: the ship was outfitted, crew signed on, orders were
given and obeyed, kicks were meted out and buttocks received kicks, the anchor weighed, salty songs were sung,
sweet melancholy touched the air, a great huzzah! went up
and we were off, etc.

The Self-Advocate

As we are now fairly embarked in this business, and as my
leg—or should I say the absence of my leg—plays so great
a part in this tale, I am all anxiety to convince ye, ye ABS, of
the injustice done us crips.

In the first place, it may be deemed almost superfluous
to establish the fact that among people at large the family of
cripples is not thought one worth joining. Indeed, when a
child is spat from its mother's womb, the first two questions
heard are: "Boy or girl?" and "Is it all right?" No practitioner
of the midwife's art ever stands beaming above the mother
and proclaims, "What a fascinating child you've given birth
to! Six-fingered!" or "Legs fused into a fin! A veritable mer-
man!" Nay!

Allow me, as a brief aside, to allude to a passage in Ishmael's version of this text in which he makes much of the
Sperm Whale having no nose. One might equally make the
argument that he is little save nose, that his whole vast head

is homologous to that part of us that goes before us into the world. So, too, if a man has no leg, the world can see little of him save that leg which is not there.

Aye, more than one of us has a tale to tell of sitting on a corner, dressed for success, waiting to board a bus, holding a cup of Starbuck's, and having a quarter tossed into it. A filthy quarter, germ-ridden by the hands of the tossing philanthropist, ruining our $3.95 coffee, not to mention our silk suit!

But are we worthy of this pitying contempt in which we are generally held?

Consider, ye ABS, this: we do ye, if I may make so bold, the inestimable service of making ye normal.

Well, after pondering that statement for some time ye may it to me concede, but still ye say:

The crip no place in myth.

The crip no place in myth? Did not the ancient Greeks have a gimp sitting atop Mount Olympus, the own dear brother of Zeus? Did not the Romans, when they recycled the Greeks' gods, import wholesale this selfsame Hephaestus and dub him Vulcan, the finest celestial mechanic who ever lived? Did not the ancient Nordic lays tell that the gods would be led out to battle on the last day by a one-eyed god, Odin, followed by blind Hoder and one-armed Tyr? Do not tourists to this day bring back from the Pueblos sterling silver pins and T-shirts bearing the image of the magnificently endowed and hunchbacked Kokopelli? Did not the Egyptians worship a dwarf god, Bes?

The crip no famous author, and cripdom no famous artists? Who wrote the first account of Hephaestus? Who but mighty Homer, himself blind! And who our greatest poet after Mr. Shakespeare? Why, blind John Milton. And in my own century of origin, Monsieur Proust was by his asthma-laden lungs "impaired in a major life function"—if I may be forgiven this bureaucratese—to wit, breathing. I could mention fit-shaken van Gogh, dwarf Toulouse-Lautrec, and mad Miss Woolf . . . I'll stop there before the ABS start to squirm in their seats.

True enough, but then crips themselves are poor devils; they have no good blood in their veins.

No good blood in their veins? They have something better than royal blood there. Look to the signing of the Declaration of Independence. What see you? A one-legged man, and another who adds a palsied scrawl. Who raised this nation up from the depths of her Depression? Why a man with a pair of legs liked cooked spaghetti.

The crip never figured in any grand imposing way? Well, if I may be permitted to be so immodest as to speak of mine own accomplishments, never was there a figure that so captured the American literary imagination as myself. Ishmael? Bah, the teller of the tale is but a wan presence, while I, raging at the blank inscrutable universe, commanding my flock of able-bodied seamen to follow me, follow me recklessly on, standing athwart the deck, the Great, Castrated Father, omnipotent and frail, the emblem of my loss on full display in my abbreviated seagoing pantaloons, wearing my heart on my sleeve, so to speak, I proclaim to all and sundry that the white phallus is but a paper tiger. (Oh, but what a roar!)

But if, in the face of all this, you still declare that cripping has no aesthetically noble associations connected with it, then am I ready to shiver fifty lances with you there and unhorse you with a split helmet every time.

And, as for me, if, by any possibility, there be any as yet undiscovered prime thing in me; if I shall ever deserve any real repute in that small but high hushed world which I might not unreasonably be ambitious of; if, at my death, my executors, or more properly my creditors, find any precious MSS in my desk, then here I prospectively ascribe all the honor and the glory to the knowledge I learned from being a gimp. This whale ship on which I was crippled was my Yale College and my Harvard, complete, I tell you, with a disability studies program, a culturally diverse faculty, and a queer studies department.

The Quarter-Deck

From New Bedford we had set out and, as you may recall from my antagonist's tome, I made no appearance until we were well at sea. It is a silly game we captains must play; methinks I am akin to Oz's Wizard in that I must conceal myself behind an elaborate deceitful drapery.

Consider ye this: I—or perhaps, to be more honest, it is the unseen Hand of Capital working its will through me— asks of my men to set out to sea; to leave behind the dear solidity of land; to leave behind the soft hands and sweet smells of women; to partake of naught but hardtack, gruel, and brined meat till, if the Devil would be so good as to make an offer, they would gladly barter their eternal souls for a mess of collard greens; to risk their lives for the death of the whale; to know that they might ne'er return to port. Moreover, our old friend, the Mighty Dollar, decrees that these hands receive but poor financial recompense for their works and pains.

So how then do we motivate—to use your contemporary parlance—our men to sail with us? To answer this question we must turn not just to Marx but to Gramsci (whom, I may here add, we are proud to number in our Confederacy of Crips). That is to say, we needs must speak of the terrible economic forces that pushed our men to sea but also of how the men's consent was manufactured. To so do, I, the captain, must pretend that this is something more than a pursuit of money, cold hard cash, filthy lucre, the needful. Just as the Crusades hid their true purpose of economic domination under the veil of the quest for the Holy Grail, so, too, must our voyage become a Noble Cause.

And so one day I, at last, ascended the cabin gangway to the deck. There, as do most sea-captains at that hour, I walked the deck, as country gentlemen, after the morning meal, take a few turns in the garden.

An art there is to such a walk: one must not stroll but tread and on one's face fix a gaze and furrow one's brow as if engaged in monomaniacal thought. Oh, it was a fine performance I put on, pacing from binnacle to mainmast and mainmast to binnacle.

And chanced I then to overhear, as I trod past, seemingly in my own thoughts deeply mired, Stubb whispering to Flask, "D'ye mark him, Flask? The chick that's in him pecks against the shell. 'Twill soon be out."

I spent the day a-pacing; now above decks, now below, till it drew near dusk. "Starbuck!" I bellowed then. "Send everybody aft."

"Sir?" said he, for such an order was only in extraordinary circumstances given.

"Send everybody aft. Mastheads, there! Come down!"

Gathered they all there in front of me, but I then ignored them and continued my heavy turns upon the deck. If I may immodestly say, I gave quite a masterful performance and had them in my thrall ere ever I spoke my first words. Then, seeming to start myself out from a trance, I spoke: "What do ye do when ye see a whale, men?"

"Sing out for him!"

"Good!" I cried. "And what do ye next, men?" Like the one whose job it is to warm up the audience before a quiz show, I understood that I must get them shouting, and get them shouting in unison, too.

"Lower away and after him!" they rejoined, as one.

"And what tune is it ye pull to, men?"

"A dead whale or a stove boat!"

We were all intoxicated, and we intoxicated one another.

"All ye mast-headers have before now heard me give orders about a white whale. Look ye! d'ye see this Spanish ounce of gold? It is a sixteen dollar piece, men. D'ye see it?" And, having commanded Mr. Starbuck to fetch me a top-maul that I might hammer the coin to the mast, I commenced giving great attention to this coin, polishing it upon my jacket whilst at the same time making a low hum to myself.

"Whosoever of ye raises me a white-headed whale with a wrinkled brow and a crooked jaw; whosoever of ye raises me that white-headed whale, with three holes punctured in his starboard fluke—look you, whosoever of ye raises me that same white whale, he shall have this gold ounce, my boys!"

"Huzzah! Huzzah!" cried the men in one voice.

"Captain Ahab," now said Tashtego, a Gay Head Indian and our harpooner. "That white whale must be the same that some call Moby Dick."

Then shouts I: "Moby Dick? Moby Dick? Do ye know the white whale then, Tash?"

And one by one the harpooneers commenced to speak, discoursing on his manner of fan-tailing, his way of spouting, and the punctures in his flank.

"Aye," I shouted back after each comment. "Aye. Aye."

Then spoke Starbuck—as if on cue, although I had confided in no one the workings of my plan—"Captain Ahab, I have heard of Moby Dick—was it not Moby Dick that took off thy leg?"

I showed myself all aquiver, as if found out. "Who—who told you that?" Then, after a pause, "Aye, Starbuck, aye, my hearties all around: it was Moby Dick who dismasted me," and saying this, I gave off an animal sob. Oh, Brando, Bernhardt, De Niro: I put them all to shame. "Aye, aye! and I'll chase him round Good Hope and round the Horn and round the Norway Maelstrom and round perdition's flames before I give him up. And this is what ye have shipped for, men! to chase that white whale on both sides of land and over all sides of earth, till he spout black blood and rolls fin out. What say ye, men, will ye splice hands on it, now?"

And "Aye," they shouted back. "Aye! Aye!"

"God bless ye," I said, with much dramatic effect. "God bless ye, men. Steward! Go draw the great measure of grog." And then I cast my eye on Starbuck and noticed his grim demeanor. Ah, he plays his role as if I had coached him on it. "But what's this long face about, Mr. Starbuck; art thou not game for Moby Dick?"

And now Starbuck, all right angles and rectitude, chided me: dry Starbuck, Quaker Starbuck, hard as a twice-baked biscuit Starbuck, render-unto-Caesar-that-which-is-Caesar's

Starbuck: "I am game for the crooked jaw of Moby Dick, and for the jaws of Death, too, Captain Ahab, if it fairly comes in the way of business; but I came here to hunt whales, not my commander's vengeance. Thy vengeance will not fetch much in our Nantucket market." Not the glittering Spanish dollar but the crisp freshly minted greenback should we chase!

"Nantucket market! Hoot!" says I. "Is the world now made of guineas and the accountants the new popes who divvy it up?" I glared Starbuck down until he retreated into the counting house of his bosom and locked the door from inside.

"The measure! The measure!" cried I then. And like a Communion cup we of the grog each partook, swearing to each other vows of fealty, and pledged, "Death to Moby Dick! God hunt us all, if we do not hunt Moby Dick to his death!"

The Absence of the Leg

(Ruminations overheard)

I, being captain, shout aloud what I have to say; but Ishmael, having no such exalted position, can only stand at the rail and murmur his thoughts to the wind. (Recall Ms. Parker's quip: A girl's best friend is her mutter.)

"What is it about that absent leg that so disarms me? How can I even hope to articulate these thoughts, when these thoughts are like miasmic gas? Yet put them into some form I must, or they will drive me mad as Ahab.

"Is it the mechanical aspect of it which me appalls? The fact that a bone of whale is substituted for a human bone?

But don't we mark it a great difference between ourselves and the rest of the animal kingdom that we are makers of tools, that while the great ape may curl up 'neath the branches of a tree she happens upon, we build shelters for ourselves? How, then, should we not think the man who fashions for himself a leg of whale more fully human rather than less?

"Logic decrees that it should be so, but there is something in me that logic cannot touch.

"How is it that sometimes that leg appears to be leering at me? I know it wants me, as surely as I know that a thing cannot want.

"Oh, I do not understand. My reason seems to be about to grasp hold of it, but while my fingers can graze it, I cannot grab it. My mind is like a caged bird—it beats its wings against its wire prison trying to be free of this thing.

"There is something powerful queer at work here."

The White Leg

What, then, did young Ish know of my white leg? He had gathered the bare outlines of the story on the deck, but I knew that much is made when little is said; and that beneath the deck, out of my earshot, that white leg took on a nearly legendary cast.

Two legs have I: one of bone, muscle, blood, and that flesh custom has decreed we call white, although if you lay the hand of a white man or white woman on a white sheet of paper it is clear that White is not white; ah, but my other leg, that is indeed white. Perhaps that is part of what so riles them about this leg of mine. For the white race had been told that we have dominion over other, darker races; and the sign of heaven's favor is the paleness of our skin. Yet when whiteness is whitened, it ceases to be White and becomes merely white.

And further, when we stare at the amputated stump, at what are we staring? How can nothingness so enthrall us? Is it that it recalls the abyss from which we all came and to which we all return?

Surely these associations and thoughts tumbled through young Ish's mind, as they did in some manner with all the men. And yet, for this young one, who made it clear he was no ordinary seaman, these troubl'd musings took on added import: he was like a dog with a bone, with that bone leg of mine.

The other men did not ship out because they had grown grim about the mouth and found themselves bringing up the rear of funerals; they weren't given to getting their feet stuck in philosophic quagmires; these other ship hands had been born in bawdy houses or on failing family farms; their mothers had stuck a gin-soaked rag in their mouths as a substitute for their teats or passed them to their older sisters, only slightly out of infancy themselves, to rear; these men had known not just the soul's hunger but the body's; they had reached satori one night in a tavern in the Brooklyn dockyards; these men, Ish, my boy, didn't get themselves all tangled up in what isn't there. What does my leg mean? What, pray tell, AB sisters and brothers, does your leg mean? To these questions the ordinary seamen respond with Zen simplicity: We know that in heaven there is no beer, so certainly there won't be any in hell: so pass the bottle, mate.

Ish wants to be a man among men, to stand shoulder to shoulder with others whose bodies give off the rank sweetish odor of old sweat and cheap tobacco, not to be the effete son of a merchant, not to be gawky and odd: he wants to pre-figure Hemingway and Mailer—to be a drinker, a carouser, a roustabout, a whorer, a sot, a mutineer; he wants to for-get all his bookish l'arning, everything his mother and his schoolmarms taught him. But oh, how he's revolted at the smell of the meat served aboard ship, how the sight of flog-ging brings tears to his eyes; he can't stand to think that he will live out his life without some sense of Purpose. He's got to make something of everything; he's got to make some-thing of that whalebone leg of mine: he don't know what else to do with it.

Business, Narrative and Otherwise

And so, with the men's souls forged to mine, we continued on our voyage until one day from the crow's nest we heard Tashtego give the call: "There she blows! There! There! There! She blows! She blows!"

And then it was all shouts: "Lower away! Lower away!" "Ready! Ready!" "Spread yourselves, boys," for we were by then in the water. "Pull, pull, my children." "Break your backbones, my boys." "Oh, ye ragamuffin rapscallions, pull!" And after the whale we were, and all the gloominess of that endless sea, which had but lately set us to finding it akin to the vast expanse of featureless eternity that everywhere surrounds us, was suddenly alive, a carnival of destruction. A squall was coming up; we fought the squall and the squall fought us; in our boats we chased the whale and the *Pequod* chased us and Death seemed to chase us all.

But we did not perish; only whales perished. We had

crossed the blear Atlantic to the Azores; we now skirted that string of islands called the Cape Verdes; we then sailed down the coast of Africa to the Cape of Good Hope. The mood of the ship was sometimes made dreary by the grayness of the sky and the grayness of the sea, causing each of us to retreat inside himself; in the sunny south sea climes, we were gay as the swabbies aboard the HMS *Pinafore*.

Were I not forced by circumstance to speak to you in this truncated form, I would at as great length as did the first scribbler of this tale set down my version of what unfolded during those long months at sea—and with as much verbal facility (nay, more) I, too, would have writ on the sea ravens and the albatross or gooney bird, regaled you with a tale of far more interest than the Town-Ho's Story; with what tender honesty I would have described the marital bed of the whales and the scene of the nursing calves. But the *Pequod* did not set sail for the sake of wandering about the globe: no, it had an end, a Final Purpose. Its aim was not my vengeance on a dumb brute nor a chance for melancholic young men to wax philosophic nor a place for the below-decks cavorting of randy lads; its aim was not even the lighting of lamps and the cinching of female waists with whalebone stays: no, its aim was to take living things and turn them into dollars, and for all that I might stand on the deck and shout at dour Starbuck, "Hoot on the Nantucket Market!" still, for that end we sailed and slaughtered. So, too, this story has an aim, and just as it is not permitted to return to the port from whence we set out and say to the bankers and widows and other investors who greet us at the dock, "Oil? Ambergris?" and strike our foreheads with our palms, "Why, we were so busy thinking about how meditation is wedded to water and pondering the philosophic import of whiteness we plum forgot! Hey, Starbuck, we forgot the whale oil!" as if we'd come back from Safeway without the milk. No, we must come to an ending, we must gather up the scattered threads, we must roll on towards an inevitable conclusion much as a human life rolls on inevitable towards death. Cash, sisters; cash, brothers: cash, cash, cash!

But first, time out for this:

The Dirty Part

Pay no attention to the story told; mark the story not told!

What Ishmael could write of only in hints and intimations, I can, in this more frank age in which we now find ourselves, write of with far greater candor. Do ye think that, finding ourselves at sea for months stretching into years, we maintained a chaste demeanor and knew each other not? No, we were not monks. Now when Ishmael penned his tale, he could not speak of this except obliquely: thus he told of the fearsome hierarchy of the officer's dining table, whereat Flask recalled his days when he was a common man before the mast and could fist a bit of old-fashioned beef in the forecastle: but we know that one kind of orifice represents another, and the same can be said for appetite.

And need I tell you that the captain is a lonely man? The ship sails to a warm clime and the men, while carrying out their labors, strip their torsos bare and are sheened with sweat; if the day be particularly warm, they draw up buckets of water and toss them upon each other, which makes them appear as good as naked. (Idle hands being the devil's playground, I set them to swabbing and polishing every bit of the gimcrackery which adorned the ship, till we would have held our ground against the most house-proud of Nantucket housewives.) The captain's flesh is pale, for it would not be seemly for him to strut about bare-chested; while the ship men's arms grow thick and muscled from hauling rig and swabbing decks, the sole exercise the captain gets is moseying along the deck, his hands clasped behind his back and stroking his chin.

I am one whose affections have always been most catholic. Aye, let it be known that whilst among the feminine I find myself drawn to sunny girls with rosy cheeks and blond hair, when a lad catches my eye he is wont to be gaunt and dark, with several days' worth of beard, at least, and a melancholy mien.

I count myself no more vain then most men, but probably, too, no less. It is a fact that when a man reaches the age I then was and he finds a lad some two decades his junior lapping about his heels like a puppy dog, he will be in some wise flattered.

But did I delude myself? Ish was fascinated by me; he feared me; he feared his fascination. My absent leg to him was like the head of old Medusa: it aroused in him a simultaneous dread and desire, a yearning of and hatred for something he dared not look on and yet must look on.

Oh, but what is love but obsession wrapped up in a pretty bow? It may be just as apt to say he hated me. Aye, more apt.

But he could not take his eye from me; he could not get enough of the part of me that was not there. My blank leg was like his own face: the part to us most dear, yet the part Fate keeps us ever from knowing save in dim reflection.

'Twas as if his fascination with my kind was immutably de-creed. What found he when he went searching for a place to lodge in New Bedford? Why, a house to stay in that was—palsied. And that text of his, lurching first this way, then that, misshapen, deformed, totally lacking in any sense of pleasing wholeness or symmetry—it is as crippled as the Co-logne Cathedral with its mismatched spires. Ish told you he loves to sail forbidden seas and land on barbarous coasts. He made of me his forbidden sea, his barbarous land. Aye, he had been looking for me ere ever he laid his piercing eye on me. He had been looking for me ere this poor place we call the universe was formed.

And then one day when we were off the coast of Japan, having been at sea for some six months, Ish and I chanced to find ourselves alone on deck when our first—and only—physical intimacy occurred.

It was a kiss.

Oh what a democratic device is the kiss! I have a mouth, thou hast a mouth, she or he has a mouth, ye have mouths—we all have mouths. In this act two bodies connect, not as male and female, not as top and bottom, but in perfect, egalitarian harmony. Would it not be a good thing for this fragmented Nation of ours if, encountering each other on city streets and in rural post offices, on underground trains and in supermar-ket lines, we turned to the stranger next to us and bussed their lips? Hath not a Jew arms, legs? asks Will. Well, frankly, sweet William, some do not. But in all my travels through this world of the impaired, while I have met some with palsied tongues and quivering lips, I have never met man or woman lacking that sublimely hermaphroditic organ, the mouth! Let us away then with this lovely democratic tumble of the tongues!

Yet the man seeking intimacy at sea faces an odd conundrum. What is the ocean upon which he sails? True enough, it is the vast amniotic fluid of the world itself, a womb wherein we all were stewed into being; but it is a grave, too. Think ye on all the countless millions of organisms that have graced this world with their presence: most have made the ocean both their home and their final bed. From the lowly amoeba to the regal walrus, the dugong and the manatee, the anchovies that swim in great schools, the smelt and sprat, sea anemones and kelp, lobster, octopus, and squid, all are decayed into the ocean brine. We not only sail upon the plantation and the cemetery of plankton and of krill, of the mighty shark and of the mightier whale: the very atoms of the dead are inextricably mixed, part of the spray that saturates the air, of the salt water with which we wash.

When we pressed lip to lip, Ishmael and I, we felt not only a nervous tingle but also the taste of death.

Oh, that kiss! We seek to break out of the prison of the body, to have our ethereal soul touched by another, but the filthy body—unbathed for months save with the spray of seawater, the mouth a cave filled with ferment—demands that we make our way to the soul through it!

The ship itself, I'll warrant, is the perfect microcosm of poor humanity's lot. We stand on the deck and look out at the endless vistas of the infinite gray sky and the infinite gray sea; this singular sight sends us pondering eternal nirvanic emptiness. We shudder to know that we are a solitary quark, space stretching dimensionless all around us. And beneath decks? What we wouldn't give for a fragment of that infinite expanse. We bow our heads, not to any cosmic notions but to the profane fact of the deck boards above our heads. That bliss of masculine marriage, when men yoke themselves together at their above-deck labors, finds its counterpart in the stifling horror of the mass-marital bed where, netted up in their hammocks like so many caught fish, the men sway, giving off their pestilential night odors, farts that stink of hardtack, oatmeal, and cured meats. The smell of the hold makes you yearn for the sharp smell of sulfur and brimstone, searing nostrils clean!

And then there was the sound of footsteps on the foredeck ladder, our embrace broke itself off.

For some weeks thereafter he seemed to be avoiding me. I am not given to calling one of the men under me on some pretext to my cabin there to press an unwanted suit on him. If he wished to steer clear of me, so be it: to steer clear as if I were a fearsome iceberg in the northern sea, an iceberg that would wreck him ere he drew too close.

Ah, but that doltish, loutish stare of his! I care not what the learned professors of optics may say: that the eye is merely a passive receiver, that it gives off no vapors, no humors, that it can only be penetrated by light, never penetrate. I tell you, I could feel him staring at me, feel the laser beam of his eye on my flesh. I whipped around, caught him looking: he darted his eye away, like a naughty lad caught with his hand in the cookie jar. Oh, he was concocting something in that brain of his. He looked and looked and looked—and I had not even the privacy of skin! There my whalebone leg was, exposed, naked, plain, bone-white.

The Squeezing of the Sperm

Well, we went on about our business; to wit, the business of turning things which lived and swam and dove and nursed their babes, objects strange and mysterious, into objects without mystery, into things that are worth so many dollars, cash on the barrel. A dead whale is just so much blubber and dead meat fit for sea dogs: it must be tried into products, and I must become not just a captain but a factory boss.

And so one day I was at the helm, holding a steady course, trolling out my nine fathoms an hour. The men under my command were busying themselves round a vat which held the sperm of a whale that had been cooled and crystallized to such a degree that it was necessary to squeeze the lumps therein back into liquid. Ishmael was one of the crew I assigned to this task: he sat himself down on the deck, cross-legged like a Hindoo, much to the amused derision of his fellows, and began to squeeze. The ship, under a blue tranquil sky, was gliding serenely along; as the men squeezed, the globules discharged all their opulence, like fully ripe grapes their wine; we sniffed up that uncontaminated aroma—literally and truly like the smell of spring violets.

Oh, what a paradise there was in that task. I drew near to it, as to a musky meadow. I broke rank, cast aside my fearsome solitude, and joined the men in their squeezing. I almost began to credit the old Paracelsan superstition that sperm is of rare virtue in allaying the heat of anger; while bathing in that bath of sperm I felt divinely free from my rancor at Ish for his infernal, boorish staring; I cast off all ill-will or petulance, or malice of any sort whatsoever.

Squeeze! squeeze! squeeze! I squeezed that sperm till I myself almost melted into it; I squeezed that sperm till a strange sort of insanity came over me, and I found myself unwittingly squeezing my co-laborers' hands in it, mistaking their hands for the gentle globules. The selfsame sensibility seemed to o'ertake us all, such an abounding, affectionate, friendly, loving feeling did this avocation beget; that at last I was continually squeezing their hands, and looking up into their eyes sentimentally; as much as to say—Oh! my dear fellow beings, why should we longer cherish any social acerbities, or know the slightest ill-humor or envy! Come; let us squeeze hands all around; nay, let us all squeeze ourselves into each other. It seemed that Ish and I might cease to exist in our separate skins; our very globules of flesh might merge in some universal soup.

I do not expect that I shall be so happy again until I am laid beneath the ground and sleep in happy fellowship with a graveyard of diverse comrades—blissfully, all one and one all.

But then Ish squeezed my finger, thinking it a globule of coagulated sperm. He stared moonily up. In that moment there was no division between us: not the divisions between those with hair of gray and hair untouched by time; not the division of rank; not the division of our diverse tempers; not even, for a moment, that fearsome division of our skin. And then his face changed its mien: as sudden and swift as a South Seas squall comes up, his face became all beclouded. He dropped my hand, started back: I was not some undifferentiated, universal stuff but myself, a man apart, with my own peculiar body, my own smells, my own own-ness, my own absent leg.

Moby Dick

In the face of this, what might I have done? Shut my soul to all but its own society? But what man can make of himself a thing entirely apart? I am not a whale; I do not breach, solitary and splendid, regally indifferent to the water in which I swim, to poor humanity. I am a man; it is the nature of my soul to mingle with other souls; my fellows are my quadrant and my compass.

And so when ye dare to tremble in my presence, my heart cries out: I'll give ye reason enow to tremble! Look away from me in shame? I'll become a very machine for the making of shame!

Was I made mad by him? Was I Jim Jones, some other mad pastor bewitching myself as I my flock bewitched?

Mad?

Nay!

Emotionally disturbed?

Aye, that.

For how could I not be disturbed? Doth not the great serene Pacific find her vast waters agitated, e'en sent wild, by a gale-force wind? How, then, could we expect of a man that he be grander and more placid than the mighty ocean? Flog me with your shameful whip and think that I shall not even flinch? Only a man who has never known the lash in any form could expect such magnanimity. Did not our Lord himself on the cross writhe, flail, moan, cry out that he was bereft?

And my heart filled with a monomania and a species of horrible delight. In every life, sisters and brothers, something must be chased: be it a Spanish sixteen-dollar piece or the greenback dollar, a whale, nirvana, a place in the literary pantheon, justice; I do not fancy myself so fine a fellow that on my very deathbed I will not chase after one more breath; and then please, dear God, having given me that one, give me just one more.

So I made of myself the thing they made of me: I chased the whale, the mighty whale, the whale who had dismasted me. I chased Moby Dick. I chased him as though nothing in heaven or earth meant what that chase meant; I chased him to my peril, and the peril of my men.

And then one night, at last, mid-watch, I smelled that smell which is a sort of calling card for the Sperm Whale. How can I best describe it? Let me say that it is the odor of the sea but the sea condensed, boiled down, reduced to its essence. I sniffed the air and reset our course slightly.

And then I saw him and gave a loud cry: "Thar she blows! 'Tis Moby Dick! Thar she blows!"

Soon all the boats were manned, all dropped, all the boat sails set, all the paddles plying; with rippling swiftness, shooting to leeward, and I, I led the flock. And through the calm tropical waters Moby Dick moved on, concealing his magnificent bulk as an iceberg reveals but a small portion of itself above the waves. To see Moby Dick moving was to see a mountain move, and perhaps that suggests a tearing asunder, a rain of soil and stones, a quaking of the earth—yet despite vast bulk and his great speed his motion was in no wise cumbersome; he did glide most regal and smooth.

But soon the forepart of him slowly rose from the water; for an instant his whole marbleized body formed a high arch and, warningly waving his bannered flukes in the air, the grand god revealed himself, sounded, and went out of sight. Hoveringly halting and dipping on the wing, the white seafowls longingly lingered over the agitated pool that he left.

With oars apeak and paddles down, the sheets of their sails adrift, our three boats now stilly floated, awaiting Moby Dick's reappearance.

Tashtego was the first to spy the white birds that had surrounded the whale, which were turning towards my boat
and had begun to flutter over the water there. But suddenly,
as I peered down and down into its depths, I saw a white
living spot no bigger than a white weasel with wonderful
celerity uprising and magnifying as it rose, till it turned, and
then there were plainly revealed two long crooked rows of
white, glistening teeth, floating up from the undiscoverable
bottom. It was Moby Dick's open mouth and scrolled jaw!

And yet the great White Whale seemed strangely oblivious of our advance—as the whale sometimes will—and we
were in the smoky mountain mist that, thrown off from the
whale's spout, curled round his great Monadnock hump;
then darted I my fierce iron. And Moby Dick sideways
writhed; spasmodically rolled his high flank against the bow,
and was taken.

Yes, Moby Dick was caught, as thousands of nameless le-
viathans before him had been captured and thousands after
him would be. He was tried out: of his bones were corset
stays made; his whale oil a flame did light—a flame that died
ere you, dear reader, were ever born. Moby Dick became,
as millions—aye, billions—of living things have become,
naught but a commodity, worth so many dollars, cash on the
barrel, in the Nantucket market. His blood and bile became
so many greenbacks, and those dollars were exchanged for
other dollars, which were exchanged for other cold commodities, and so on, as the drops of water in the ocean mingle and
become indistinguishable; and mayhap some remnant of old
Moby finds himself in your change purse now.

What? This, then, is the ending of our tale? A dead whale?
A once-magnificent creature tried down into blubber and

oil and ladies' corsets? A solitary ship tacking across a vast, becalmed, dull Pacific? A pocketful of loose change? A crip who is neither cured nor dies? This the ending to the tale?

The Drama's Done

That night e'er our labors were done, after those great, infidel doings of stripping the whale of its flesh had been carried out, after the ship had become an abattoir—or mayhaps an altar to a pagan god—we celebrated the day's hunt with a feast of grog and whale meat. In profane Communion, we ate the flesh of the one we had both hunted and worshipped. The measure of grog was most liberally passed, and with great, good gluttony we unashamedly grew thick and dopey with both the liquor and the meat. In that wild feast we dined on our enemy: that is to say, he became us, and in he becoming us, we became him. We lurched about with drunken footsteps on the deck, yet still slick with blood, as our frail ship lurched upon the drunken sea. In that happy carnival we no longer knew divisions of rank or temperament: we were as one—save one.

Young Ish held himself aloof.

He had taken his old familiar place at the rail and was once again to be seen muttering, muttering to the wind: "Moby Dick dead and Ahab alive! It cannot be! And yet—it is! Moby Dick dead! The old man alive!"

Some days later I happened to espy him again. That gloomy aspect and melancholy mien that he had heretofore cultivated as a sort of sham, no longer seemed an affectation. Indeed, it seemed some monomania had got hold of him. At his labors he seemed always to be muttering, and when

I chanced to put myself within earshot of his mumblings I heard, "A mighty book—a mighty theme! . . . Science! Curse thee, thou vain toy; and cursed be all the things that cast man's eyes aloft to that heaven . . . Fate the handspike. Yes, the handspike. Oh! . . . Whiteness. Fearsome albino!" and then, his mood seeming to turn, he would sing out, "Such a funny, sporty, gamey, jesty, jokey, hokey-pokey lad is the Ocean, oh!" and dance a little jig whilst still at his labors.

This was but the least of the strange monomania that had taken possession of him. He had contrived to fashion himself, out of the quill of an albatross, a pen, and from some substances he had begged from the ship's surgeon he made himself ink, and commenced to scribble on any scribbleable surface that could be found, no mean task aboard a whaler, which is not fitted out in any wise for penmen or for scholars. Still, he managed to get a bit of old newspaper here, an envelope that had once held a letter there (and what he traded for this I can only imagine), and in a hand so quaint and fine it itself seemed obsession incarnate, he wrote and wrote and wrote.

Did I know then what it was he was at? An inkling had I, so that a century and a half later when I was "rescued" from my South Seas atoll—a portion of the tale I must here skip over—and found myself repatriated to Nantucket, and there entered a bookseller's shop, and discovered on a rustic table (rustic out of a Pottery Barn catalogue, you understand) a thick tome entitled *Moby Dick*—printed on vellum paper, amply illustrated with woodcuts—souvenirs for those whose refined tastes kept them from purchasing miniature lobster pots and plastic scrimshaw—I found between its covers only dreadful confirmation.

Ish could not cease his fearsome meaning making. The sky must fill with portents, the waves and krill must speak to him, the very brine shrimp must shout hosannas or chant kaddish; this whole vast insensible universe must be turned into a machine for making sense. Yes, my White Leg must be made to bleed meaning, if it could not bleed blood, till it strode before him in the monomaniac incarnation of all those malicious agencies which some deep men feel eating them. All that maddens and torments; all that stirs up the lees of things; all truth with malice in it; all that cracks the sinews and cakes the brain; all the subtle demonisms of life and thought; all evil, to poor Ishmael, were visibly personified, and made practically assailable in the White Leg. He piled on my white stump the sum of all the general rage and hate felt by his whole race from Adam down; and then, as if his chest had been a mortar, he burst his hot heart's shell upon it.

His thoughts had created a creature in him, and that creature was me.

Shouldst thou beware Ahab, Ishmael?

No, lad, beware thyself!

Beware thyself, Ishmael!

FINIS

In the Prairie Schooner Book Prize in Fiction series

Last Call: Stories
By K. L. Cook

Carrying the Torch: Stories
By Brock Clarke

Nocturnal America
By John Keeble

The Alice Stories
By Jesse Lee Kercheval

Our Lady of the Artichokes and Other Portuguese-American Stories
By Katherine Vaz

Call Me Ahab: A Short Story Collection
By Anne Finger

To order or obtain more information on these or other University of Nebraska Press titles, visit www.nebraskapress.unl.edu.